SISTERS

DARKNESS CANNOT DRIVE OUT DARKNESS;
ONLY LIGHT CAN DO THAT.
HATE CANNOT DRIVE OUT HATE;
ONLY LOVE CAN DO THAT.

MARTIN LUTHUR KING JR.

SISTERS

MICHAEL EDWIN Q.

Published by: ADVANTAGE BOOKS™
                  Longwood, Florida, USA
                  www.advbookstore.com

Library of Congress Catalog Number: 2021937311

1.   Fiction:: African American - Woman
2.   Fiction: African American – Historical
3.   Social Science - Slavery

Cover Design: Alexander von Ness
Editor: nancysabatinicopyedit@gmail.com

First Printing: May 2021
21 22 23 24 25 26   10 9 8 7 6 5 4 3 2 1
Printed in the United States of America

One

Choices

Something was wrong. Everything was wrong. The world was spinning out of control.

All her life led her up to this moment; however, none of it made any sense. How could someone go from being a God-fearing woman, reading the Bible, praying day and night, following the Golden Rule, become a murderer?

Well, not quite a murderer, at least not yet. The only thing needed was to pull the trigger, which she was certain she was going to do. That's what scared her. She knew without a doubt she was going to pull the trigger. She delighted in the idea. She found pleasure in it.

At least, there was no begging for mercy. That would make things harder, although not impossible.

"Do you want to pray before I kill you?"

"You still believe in that mumbo jumbo?" she laughed

"You should try to get right with the Lord, before I send you to him. You've done much evil in your life."

"True, but I've never killed anyone."

Those words cut the deepest.

"Go on, I'm waiting. Go ahead, pull the trigger."

A long silent moment took hold of them, constricting the breath from their bodies.

"You're not going to kill me," she said, sounding amused.

"Why won't I?"

"Because I know your type; I know you. I remember when first seeing you, I said, 'There's another sad eyed country girl'. Just look at you, I'd say you haven't changed much since your early days as a young girl on a plantation. I know your type. You're one of those holier-than-thou sorts. Butter wouldn't melt in your mouth. Looking down your nose at all of us sinners, only, now you see you're no different from the rest of us. You're capable of murder, as much as the next person. Except, in your mind you don't realize it, you're still on a spiritual quest. So, you won't kill me. You think you're a saint, well, saints don't kill people."

Her argument seemingly fell on deaf ears.

5

"You know, if you kill me, they'll hang you!"

"I've cheated death many times, and you know what happened, then. I've been living on borrowed time, since. I'm prepared to die."

She pulled back on the gun hammer till it clicked into place.

"Now, wait a minute," her voice quivered, "can't we talk this over?"

"There's nothing to talk over. Unless you can perform miracles, there's nothing you can do to make it right."

"Now, wait one damn minute."

The gunshot sounded through the house like a cannon blast, echoing from room to room, and ricocheting back. She'd never fired a gun in her life. The explosion surprised and shocked her. The recoil sent her arm behind her.

The body hit the floor with a loud thud. It lay lifeless behind the desk. Blood collected around the head, slowly forming a large pool around the body. The crimson splatter was across one wall, masking the titles of the books on the shelf of another wall, and a red spray across a painting of the same woman she just killed, only when she was younger.

The guards were sure to have heard. They'd be coming soon. If she was going to do anything, she needed to do it without hesitation.

Then she thought of her choices. There were only three. She could make a run for it. Her chances of escaping were slim to none; she knew it. Even if it were possible, she'd have to move immediately. Or she could give herself up, which would surely lead to her arrested, jailed, tried, and eventually hanged. She also had the notion she might try to fight her way out. She still had five bullets. Except, she'd be outnumbered by men who knew how to use a gun far better than she, the best she could hope for was taking one or two of them with her. This she felt was a worthless gesture.

Of course, there was the strong possibility they would rush in, see their mistress laying on the floor…dead, and shoot her down. This was acceptable to her.

She heard their heavy feet trampling through the house like cattle; the pounding on the wood floor was all around, and then shots rang out.

Suddenly, as if a bolt of lightning hit her, she thought of one more unexpected alternative. She placed the gun to the side of her head.

Two

Fancy

What makes up a family? When asked, most folks would speak of relatives, family trees, and bloodlines. Blood isn't the only thing that connects people. There's a joining formed in the spirit, which can be stronger and deeper. This was the bond between Jolene and Winnie. They say you can pick your friends, yet you can't your family. However, you can pick friends to be your family.

During the first parts of their lives, each didn't even know the other existed, Jolene Fairchild and Winifred Cummings, born one year apart, and many miles away from each other.

Born into slavery, blessed or cursed, depending on your view, with beauty seldom seen that blossomed in their teens.

As desirable as these two were by black and white, rich and poor, master and slave, they remained unmolested. This was not because of any moral fortitude on anyone's part, rather it concerned greed.

A young, beautiful, black slave girl could fetch a pretty penny on the open market. The selling price would triple if she was a virgin. For this reason, slaveowners took great pains for these girls to remain pure. An improper touch by slave or freeman would mean the loss of a hand, anything worse meant certain death, and not a swift or pretty one, I might add.

If you really want to make some serious money, you sell the girl to a school that will transform her into a *Fancy*.

What is a Fancy, you ask? An interesting question, not so easily answered.

A Fancy, or Fancy Girl, and sometimes called a Fancy Lady, is a young black slave girl. She must be beautiful and untouched. Light skinned girls are the most preferred, nevertheless not compulsory. They're sent or sold to a school specializing in transforming these young girls into the perfect mistresses for wealthy, often married, white southern gentlemen.

Taking months, they teach the girls to read and write. Such an act is against the law in most Southern states, though in cases of such schools the law turns a blind eye. The girls receive instructions on grooming, fashion, etiquette, also how to conduct one's self in a conversation, as well as being a good listener.

Apart from these skills, the center of their tutoring, with the most time spent, was the ways of pleasing a man in the bedroom. This is a delicate and pressing subject to teach and learn, made more so by the fact none of it was hands-on. They were to remain untainted to be worthy of the high price the schools asked for their graduates.

Once completing their studies, they sell the girl to the highest bidder. Not at an auction, mind you, auctions are far too public. All parties involved understood it best kept secret from wives. Even women, who didn't mind their husbands having a mistress on the side, or at least willing to tolerate such behavior, didn't want such things flaunted under their noses. Auctions where they buy and sell slaves were just fine with these women, some even taking part in such auctions, although, sales of a Fancy they felt best kept hush-hush.

As well, a mistress who's kept out of sight was best. Often, a nearby apartment was where the Fancy would live. Few single men did keep their mistresses in their home, except those far and in-between, as many of the upper-crust frowned on such goings-on. Not the idea of having a mistress, mind you, that was just fine with most; it's just not something you should do in your own home.

Surprisingly, despite the hefty profit they could make, there were few schools specializing in Fancy Girls. Many states, Southern States, of course, had no more than one or two such schools, while some states had none at all. There were no schools in the Northern States, where folks looked down on such behavior. Still, it was not uncommon for a wealthy northerner to buy a mistress from said schools.

If you ask anyone in the trade they would, reluctantly or not, have to agree the finest school for Fancies would be a school owned and run by Madame Charbonneau in New Orleans.

Madame Charbonneau's girls were high priced; however, all knew that no Fancy from her school was ever returned. Customer satisfaction was her hallmark.

Three

Madame Charbonneau's Story

Madame Charbonneau was well known not only within New Orleans, but throughout the surrounding states and in certain wealthy circles throughout the South.

She was famous for owning and running the finest school for training Fancy Ladies, taking beautiful yet unsophisticated black female slaves and turning them into refined ladies, worthy of being a high-priced mistress.

Little was known about Charbonneau, although all agreed she was beautiful, wealthy, and ruthless.

Depending on your status in society, morally, that is, was how one viewed her.

To wealthy gentlemen with loose morals, she was an extraordinary woman of taste and beauty that made dreams come true.

To the rest of the world, those with at least some moral in their character looked down on her as *that sort of woman*, to be shunned at all cost and turns…the dredge of the social order.

Another reason to spurn her was she was notorious, known for being wicked and vengeful when crossed…even to the point of murder.

Other than that, little was known about her, especially about her past, although, rumors abound.

Probably because of her impeccable mastery of the French language, it was believed she was born and raised in France, the southwest of the wine country in Bordeaux. Word has it; she came from a wealthy family of wine makers for three generations.

When she migrated to New Orleans, she arrived as an already wealthy woman. Gossip was her wealth was ill-gotten. Although there is no proof to substantiate these claims, no one would deny she was the sort of person to perform atrocious deeds.

Story is she was evil as far back as her childhood, and at the age of fourteen, burned down the winery, including the family home. Her parents and siblings died in the fire.

Being the sole heir, she sold the winery and acreage for half its value. Moving to Paris, she continued to live the high life, an extravagant social life as enjoyed only by the wealthy, squandering her inheritance and ill-gotten gains.

In time, her youthful folly brought her to the door of poverty. There she accepted the marriage proposal of *Martin de Porc*, a wealthy restaurateur, sixteen restaurants in all, eight within Paris, four in Marseille, two in Arles, and two in Nice.

De Porc was much older than she, more than twice her age; she nineteen at the time. He was a scrawny, uncouth, pig of a man. She despised him; still, she would endure much to continue in the life style she'd become accustomed to.

However, he adored her, showering her with gifts daily, determined to make her happy beyond her imagination, which was vast, resolved to make all her dreams come true.

****

It happens. It was not uncommon. After all, one reason for his success was his hands-on approach to his restaurants. De Porc always traveled throughout Paris and all the other cities where his restaurants were located. He'd visit each without warning. Sampling the food, making sure all was up to his high standards.

No one could imagine the amount of food he sampled daily, let alone, in the six months of their marriage.

The doctors called it food poisoning, which was understandable for a man in his position. Perhaps it was a bad piece of meat, shellfish, it was difficult to say, although all very possible.

His young bride donned her black attire, going into morning for a full week, after which, she dressed in her brightest yellow dress, and went shopping.

To everyone's surprise, she took up the responsibility of running the restaurants, far surpassing the success of her husband. Some say this is where she honed her good business sense, which she became famous for in later years.

It was at this time she acquired her reputation. She was legendary for carousing with the underbelly of the wealthy of France, even to go as far as to be labeled a libertine, a movement that was all the rage with the affluent of Paris. There was even talk she'd become a Satanist, selling her soul to the devil.

When, where, and how she decided to leave France for New Orleans to open a school for Fancies is a mystery. Just knowing there was such a thing as a Fancy is too obscure. To learn about, and knowing there was a market for such services, an oddity in itself.

Never the less, she sold all the restaurants she inherited from her husband, for a high price. With age comes experience; with experience comes wisdom. Only a fool makes the same mistake twice.

Using her maiden name, she bought her mansion, sight unseen. She was the talk of the town, the moment she stepped off the ship onto the harbor.

She took months decorating the school, using only the finest materials, causing jealousy and envy.

In time, she began to venture out into high society. It was clear she chose to associate with only the wealthy and immoral people of the upper-class, mostly scoundrels, which repulsed and distanced the churchgoing community, which was fine with her.

She was a temptress, perusing bedmates with disregard to conventional tradition, hunting in the manner of the male of the species. Her prey was whatever caught her eye, regardless, be he white or black, too young, too old, married, and at times not even a he.

Local and state politicians became close allies, which was a wise thing to do in the business world of greased palms and blind eyes.

When the first few students came to the school, most folks thought it was hopeless. One look at these backwoods girls taken from plantations from every southern state, one would bet against it.

Madame had a plan, and was determined to succeed. She understood the world broke up into two camps...good and evil.

The evil girls were a certainty. They were worldly, enjoying the finer things in life, which was promised to them if they cooperate and finally become the mistress of a wealthy southern gentleman.

The good girls, now, that was different. These girls were in the world, but not of the world...they were spiritual in nature. Just the idea of being a Fancy and becoming some man's mistress repulsed them. They would fight tooth and nail, to the death, rather then compromise their moral standards.

These were the ones Madame had to break; and there is only one way and that is through fear. Each girl was different, having their personal fear. Once Madame learned what that fear was, she applied it till the girl shattered within, and willing to do whatever she was told.

In time, students began to graduate and be sold. Madame Charbonneau became famous for supplying the most beautiful, best behaved, obliging Fancies throughout the South. She was able to call her price, and get it. Money flowed like wine.

Madame Charbonneau's methods became legendary. Her success rate was nearly perfect. In all those years, she experienced only two failures, two girls she couldn't control.

Four

Jolene's Story

Jolene was lovely all her life, from infancy to her teens. She had what folks say and parents brag about: inner beauty as well, although, it was the outer beauty that received most of the attention. It would shock you, or perhaps not, if you could read the minds of men, both black and white, when they laid eyes on her.

She was petite with a delicate natural loveliness with soft eyes, high cheekbones. Her womanly shape came in her early teens, years ahead of other girls her age. Her skin was immaculately even and smooth, more so than others in her family, without blemish.

The flame of her beauty burned brightly for all to see, yet not nearly as intense as the fire that burned in her heart. She was a warm, sweet young woman. Sympathy and compassion poured from her like rain on everyone that came in contact with her, be it family, friend, or enemy. Always with a kind word, when help was needed, she was first to arrive and last to leave.

A devoted enthusiastic churchgoer, her faith was strong. There was innocence about her that you rarely see in folk. It was her crowning glory. Though unknown to her at the time, it would be the source of much hardship for many years. Still, even if she could foresee the future, she would never change her ways.

She was born, lived and worked on the Barnett Plantation, owned and run by Garland Barnett. This, of course, made Jolene his property to do whatever he pleased. From the moment she was able to walk while carrying something in her hands, she worked in the fields. However, as she grew, Garland knew what a gem he had in his possession, a true moneymaker.

The term Fancy was just hearsay to Garland. In no way did he have any connection with people who moved in those circles. Never owning a slave girl of Jolene's good looks, he never did pursue such a sale; it was all new to him.

He wrote letters to all the Fancy schools he knew, only, to receive replies expressing they would not buy any merchandise sight-unseen. His friends advised him to go through an agent in the slave trade. Someone who'd come to the plantation to asses the girl. If the agent was convinced there was potential, he'd buy the girl, straight out with money from his own pocket. Transport her to the school, and sell at a profit. Garland understood the need for an agent. From a friend of a friend he received a name.

This is the cue for Samuel Runt to enter our story. He was well-known in the slave trade as an agent. His specialty was traveling throughout the South, buying high quality slaves and selling them for a profit to wealthy slaveowners.

His stock and trade was large male slaves who could do the work of three, also, as breeders. Female nursemaids were always in demand, as well as cooks and domestic help. However, his highest profit came from selling attractive young female slaves. As much as there was a large market for such girls, Runt knew gentlemen of quality would never pay good money for a slave girl straight off the plantation. For this reason, he sold the girls to schools for Fancies. Let them have the headache of bringing them up to snuff.

Samuel Runt was a tall, scrawny, beanpole of a man with the features of a scarecrow. His profile was as sharp as a hatchet, coming to a point at his elongated nose. Always dressed in a black suit, he had the look of an undertaker with all the charm of a corpse.

Nevertheless, Runt knew his business. In just a few minutes negotiating with Garland Barnett, he'd purchased the slave Jolene Fairchild for one-thousand dollars, far lower than Barnett hoped for and far less than what Runt was willing to pay.

With two large bodyguards always at his beck and call, Runt transported Jolene by train to New Orleans. He sold her for a profit to a school for Fancies owned and run by Madame Charbonneau.

****

Life at the school was more than tolerable; it was comfortable and extravagant. All the girls, the students, were treated like princesses. There was nothing they couldn't have within reason, the best of food, clothing, and shelter.

The school was a large two-story mansion surrounded by high walls. The property was constantly under the watch of no less than four guards per three shifts. This was not only to keep the girls from leaving; it was to keep the world out.

Although the girls were not allowed to leave the property, they received freedom to move about the grounds as they pleased.

They received the finest foods, three times each day. It was mandatory that each student wash from head to toe every day. The wardrobe was worthy of royalty, including expensive perfumes. They were pampered in a life of luxury. There were never more than twelve students in resident, at a time. Upstairs bedrooms were spacious, clean with only two girls to a room.

Madame Charbonneau ran a tight ship, like the commander of the fleet, or a general on the battlefield. She dealt with the girls with a firm hand and an iron fist, seldom giving reward, swift with vicious punishments. There was punishment for any infraction, although it was usually nothing worse than going to your room without supper, all the way to being whipped or battered. The penalty was always at Madame's whim. In many ways they lived in a prison, except the bars were bars of gold. There was a tight hold on them, although the hands that held them falsely appeared to wear kid gloves, they were actually deadly and hurtful.

Many of the girls thought they were in heaven, and felt pleased and excited by what lay ahead for them. All were from plantations. It was a life of no prospects. They spent most their days in the fields, sweating and toiling. Being beautiful, they could expect to be raped regularly by the master, overseers, and slaves. The best she could hope for was to marry a man she didn't love, have a handful of children, and then work herself into an early grave.

The prospect of living a life in luxury was a dream come true. The downside was they would have to be the mistress of some wealthy gentleman. The upside was that it was only one man, hopefully a gentle and generous man, preferably, a much older man – easy to please. The title of mistress was far more favorable than the one of slave.

Despite all these amenities and possibilities, Jolene was the one girl who saw it all as a tragedy. In her mind it was far better to live your life out as a slave performing hard labor than an immoral life. What you sow, so shall ye reap, for her this was a recipe for disaster, if not now, then in the afterlife.

Although she felt uncomfortable, disagreeing with the lifestyle and philosophy imposed on her, she never once spoke against it. She preferred to not make waves, never once voicing her disapproval, playing the wallflower.

There was one bright light within all this darkness. Jolene's roommate was Winifred Cummings, known to all as Winnie. Both girls were each fair skinned, although, Winnie was light enough to pass for white. She confided in Jolene that she had tried to and succeeded to pass on more than one occasion. Only, reprimands from family and friends swayed her with shame of doing so.

Their philosophies of life were poles apart, Winnie with her free and adventurous spirit, Jolene with her shy demeanor and strong ethics. Still, the two became closer than close, despite the differences between them.

Like the other girls, Winnie reviled in her new life. She believed strongly in it. Looking back on the road she'd traveled, all she saw was a life of misery. The road ahead held some sense of hope. There was a light at the end of the tunnel.

Every night, she tried to enlighten Jolene to see the wisdom of being a Fancy Girl, compared with the foolishness of fighting against the inevitable.

Jolene did her best to make her point to get Winnie to see how wrong she was. The light at the end of the tunnel was coming from fire and brimstone.

In the end, neither could sway the other. They agreed to disagree.

****

Unseen by the human eye, the spirit moves. In time, Jolene and Winnie became sisters, a family to themselves, to care for and be cared for.

Taking up the responsibilities of an older sister, Winnie watched out for Jolene, her naïveté causing more harm than good. Many of the girls took advantage of Jolene's good nature. In her innocence, often Jolene held no idea they took advantage of her. That was when Winnie would step in, stand up for her, and make things right.

Eventually, the day Winnie dreamed of and worked so hard for arrived. She graduated. She was now a Fancy. She would then be sold to the highest bidder. She had no idea whose mistress she'd become, except, to her it didn't matter. She felt determined to make the best of the situation.

On her last night at the school, before being taken to her new home in the morning, Winnie lie in bed, too excited to sleep. She stared up into the darkness, counting the minutes till her good fortune. It was then fate did what it often does, it took a sharp turn from the course onto the path least expected.

Jolene's whisper traveled through the darkness, across the room to Winnie. It was a plea for help. It seemed Jolene tried to escape the night before, using a chair to scale the wall in the garden. Clearly, she failed, and was now asking for Winnie's help. Only with her aid could she escape over the wall. Jolene pleaded in tears.

"Please, Winnie, you're my only hope. Once you're gone, I will be alone. I need your help. Please!" Jolene begged.

Winnie understood what this meant to Jolene. As much as Winnie wanted a life as a Fancy Girl, Jolene feared it. She knew Jolene's heart, and that it was breaking.

Only, why of all nights this night, the eve of Winnie's start of a new life? If caught, who's to say what the punishment might be? Winnie didn't fear death, which could be the result. However, the thought of her dream dashed weight on her heavily.

"Why tonight of all nights," Winnie asked. "Do you know what you're asking of me? I've worked hard to get to this place, and now you want me to risk it all. If we're caught it'll mean back to the plantation, or worse."

They argued, Winnie desperately trying to convince Jolene to stay, Jolene pleading with Winnie to escape with her, or at least help her. In the end, neither one could convince the other.

Jolene's tears melted Winnie's heart. There was a soft spot there for Jolene, one she knew she would have for the rest of their lives. In the end, Winnie consented to help Jolene.

Stealing downstairs, they took one of the chairs from the dining room, and then outside, placing it against the garden wall.

They parted in tears, vowing to remain sisters for life.

Standing atop of the chair, Winnie helped Jolene over the wall. Winnie returned the chair and then rushed back to her room, as Jolene ran off into the night, both believing they had made the right decision and both believing they would never see each other again.

However, no one can say for sure what may or may not come. The day of the prophet has long since passed; no tarot may speak so loudly to know what's around the bend, no crystal ball so deep it heralds more than shadows. For fate holds all our lives in her hands, and she holds her hands behind her back.

****

In each life there are peaks and valleys. Peaks so high, you wish you'd never come down. Valleys so low, you cry, pleading for a way out. The balance or imbalance of these two parts of life varies from person to person. Some go through life, truly blessed with nary a worry in the world, while others feel pressed with life's weight with only glimpses of relief, if any at all. Still, nothing lasts forever, those at the zenith will at some time spend time in the valley below, while those in the valley will struggle and reach the mountaintop. And so it goes, the cycle is repeated.

Such was not the case with the adventures of Jolene. It seemed she had taken up permanent residence in the valley. Even during the moments she believed she'd immerged from the depths, she was to find out it was only false hope.

Perhaps, it was obvious innocence; still, everyone she met took advantage of her. The world was a masquerade with each person wearing the mask of falsehood. It was heartbreaking every time the veil was lifted and Jolene was confronted with the truth. All were liars. If they claimed to be a friend, they turned out to be an enemy. Swearing they cared, only to find out it was only themselves they cared about. Each act performed in self-interest, backstabbers every one of them.

And as for lovers, all were false. This was the hardest to bear. When the heart is on the line, the gamble is for your life's breath, more precious than fame or fortune. For Jolene was easy to love, yet more willing to love with such a gentle heart, so easily broken.

Anyone else would have sunk into the depths of depression, giving up on life, except Jolene. She believed every struggle, every disappointment was a gift from God, prompting her to be a better person.

****

Years passed, her life spiraling further into darkness, and then finally hitting bottom. Having falling into bad company, when crimes were committed, they all turned on her, pointing their fingers, blaming it all on her, the one and only innocent among them. Of course, she was blameless; childlike, nevertheless, justice is not only blind it is sometimes partial.

The charges were horrendous. When found guilty, there was nothing left to do, the judge held no alternative other than sentence her to death.

She spent hours waiting in her cell for the morning of her hanging.

At first light, after a sleepless night, they led Jolene to the square behind City Hall. The small crowd watched on as she climbed the stairs to the gallows. A sack over her head and a noose tight around her neck, she waited for the moment the trapdoor would be released, sending her to oblivion.

She could not foresee a reprieve; however, to her surprise they took the sack off her head and the noose from her neck. She received no reasons. They brought her back to her cell where she sat in confusion, waiting for an answer.

Hours later, they took her from her cell to the streets, and then took her to a large mansion, the home of Jonathan Gibbs, the city judge. They escorted her to a sitting room, where a handsome man greeted her. He was an elegant white man, well-groomed with striking good looks. He smiled at her, offering her a seat, as he sat across from her.

"One of the duties of a City Judge is to oversee the rulings of the Municipal Courts, here in New Orleans," he said. "They tried you in a Municipal Court. I have the jurisdiction to overturn any of their rulings, which I've done in your favor," he told her, smiling ever so gently at her.

"Why would you do that?" Jolene asked.

"Because I believe you're innocent."

"Why?" she continued.

He laughed. "To be honest, it wasn't me, it was my wife. She sat in on the trial. She listened to your accusers. She believes it was all false accusations. She believes you're not guilty. She has a way of seeing through to the truth. I trust her judgment."

Jolene was shaking, nearly in tears.

"Ah, here is my wife, now," he announced, looking to the door.

Jolene turned to see a woman approaching, a beautiful woman of elegance, dressed like a princess.

"Didn't I tell you, darling, she was innocent," she said, smiling at Jolene.

"Yes, you did, my dear," he agreed.

"Has it been that long," the woman said. "Don't you recognize your sister?"

Jolene leaned forward, taking a closer look at the woman's face.

"Winnie!" cried Jolene.

"Yes, but now it's Mrs. Gibbs. I've worried about you everyday since the night I helped you over the wall of the school. You were the sister I never had. I'm sorry about all that's happened to you. Now all that will change," She turned to Jonathan. "Can she stay with us?"

"If it makes you happy, of course she can," he said with a smile.

"Yes, it would." She took hold of Jolene's hand. "Oh, my dear sister…"

The two women hugged, holding each other in tears.

Five

Winnie's Story

Not knowing what else to do, Winifred Cummings, Winnie to friends and family, took up the name Cummings. The owner of the plantation, as well as the owner of Winnie was Terrance Cummings. He was a successful businessman, although, not a smart man. Still, he was smart enough to know he had a good thing, a moneymaker, in Winnie.

She was the loveliest girl in the county, admired by all women, lusted after by all men, young and old, black and white. Her eyes, the center of her beauty, attracted the world to her. Her family was second generation African with smooth black skin. Whereas, Winnie's skin was so light she could pass for white, which she did at times until, after being caught more than once, was punished severely for doing so, not to mention the disapproval of her family.

Terrance Cummings took pains to insure Winnie remained untouched, fully intending to sell her to the highest bidder. The problem was there were no bidders. As much as she was desirable, she was rebellious. Every potential buyer within the county and surrounding counties knew of her sassiness, disobedience, and how often she tried to run away. She was just not worth the money and aggravation. There were no takers.

Though he tried not to show his enthusiasm, Terrance Cummings was beside himself when a strange man by the name of Samuel Runt showed up with the desire and capital to purchase Winnie.

Runt worked as an agent in the slave trade for many years. Not only was he more experienced than Cummings, he was far smarter. The trick is to make your opponent believe they are superior to you and that they have bamboozled you at the game of buying and selling. Runt was a bargaining genius.

When the dust settled, Runt purchased Winnie for three hundred dollars in gold. Of course, Cummings hoped for more, although in the end he felt he'd done well to be rid of her with three hundred to boot. Little did he know Runt would have gone as high as a thousand.

****

By way of train, Runt with two of his guards took Winnie to New Orleans. There they delivered her to Madame Charbonneau's school. As wild and rebellious as Winnie could be, she behaved well, keeping to herself and obeying all the rules.

Point of interest, what caused the differences between Jolene and Winnie, both raised on a plantation, both beautiful and young, yet, they were as different as day and night.

The answer, though simple, is not easily uncovered. It comes down to influences. Jolene was raised around women of deep commitment to God, family, and community. Church and the Bible played a large part of her upbringing, from an early age up to the day she was sold.

Whereas, Winnie was never loved or taught, raising herself as best she could. She lived in a community that was dog eat dog. Her family, a small group of selfish folk, made sure they clothed and fed her, nothing more, and even that they did poorly. As for God, that was merely a word to curse with.

Many propose that it isn't necessary to believe in God to be moral. Perhaps, it can be done, although, most never find the strength to climb such a high mountain alone with only their own power and on their own cognizance.

So, when Winnie came to Madame Charbonneau's school, Winnie was a blank slate, ready to be written on by the first person to show interest in her. This would be where Lucinda enters our story.

Understandably, Lucinda was as lovely as all the other girls, a dark skinned beauty with an air about her none of the other girls possessed. It was as if Lucinda was raised differently, not on a plantation, raised by royalty.

Lucinda was Winnie's roommate, before Jolene ever came to the school. The two got along, only in the sense that they didn't quarrel, which was common among the girls. However, friendship didn't seem to be in the cards, as neither one of them believed in opening up to another person, which makes you vulnerable.

Nonetheless, in time a bond formed between them, mostly through late night talks in their room, each one in their bed, speaking across the darkness. However, it didn't start as your normal chitchat. It began as strong criticism of Winnie by Lucinda.

"You foolish girl," Lucinda said coldly, never one for mincing words.

"What do you mean?" Winnie asked, sounding defensive.

"You're not sensible; you live in a fantasy world. You trust everyone and everything. Yours is a dream world."

"What do you mean?" Winnie repeated.

Lucinda knew of Winnie's misfortunes, from her life on the plantation to the journey with Runt to the school. Winnie always tried to escape whenever she saw a possibility; and each time it was foiled by someone she gave her trust to.

"You trusted the law, when they caught you downtown. No one spoke up for you. You trusted your family and friends. Where were they when you were locked in the barn by your owner, like an animal? You trusted the hotel security on the trip here, and he turned you over to your captives. And foolishly, you trusted the Reverend Lugner to protect you. He betrayed you for a handful of silver, your own personal Judas. Worst of all, you trust God!"

"You shouldn't say things like that!" Winnie protested, not knowing why, only that it rubbed her the wrong way.

Lucinda laughed, "Where was God when you were born a slave, when they took you from your family, when they brought you here for the benefit of someone else? Your entire life has been for the benefit of someone else. There is no God. Even if there is a God, he's either powerless or he doesn't care. If you pray to this God or nothing at all, your chances of getting what you want are the same. Wake up!"

"But without God there's nothing, no morals," Winnie argued.

"And what are morals? Nothing more than laws laid down by men to keep others in line. They're as much a fantasy as your God. If you want something, you take it. If someone gets in your way, kill them. Lie, cheat, steal, whatever it takes. No one else is going to do it for you. Because, when all is said and done, you're the one who's going to lie in your grave, not them. You are your own god! You're such a foolish girl."

"I'm not a fool," Winnie bickered.

Lucinda laughed, turning onto her side, and then closing her eyes.

****

With a lifetime of no guidance, there was no base for Winnie to stand on. Lucinda's words filled her mind, directing her for the first time in her life. An empty chalice, no matter how grand, holds only what you put in it, be it sweet wine or bitter poison.

Winnie copied Lucinda in everyway, whenever possible. She took Lucinda's philosophy to heart. Winnie vowed to live for herself alone. Swept away were all her old ideas of good and evil. From then on, anything that furthered her ambitions was good.

She stole whatever she wanted. When confronted with a house infraction, she lied, often placing the blame on one of the other girls. This made her extremely unpopular. Still, what did she care?

****

Early one morning, Madame Charbonneau gathered Cora, the head matron, and the other girls into the parlor. The announcement went straight through Winnie's heart, though she refused to admit it even to herself. Lucinda was now a graduate, sold to the highest bidder. She was to leave in the morning.

Winnie watched from the upstairs window, as a most elegant carriage pulled up to the mansion. Two footmen loaded Lucinda's trunks atop. They held the carriage door for her. Winnie waved, hoping Lucinda would gaze up for one last good-bye. She entered the carriage, never looking back. Winnie watched them drive through the front gate and then out of view. Lucinda got what she always wanted.

It was not a long time later; Winnie overheard some of the girls whispering.

"What is it?" Winnie asked.

"You haven't heard? Lucinda is dead!"

Lucinda broke one of the major rules of being a mistress. She turned up pregnant. She tried to get rid of it and bled to death.

Winnie thought about it for days, till she finally came to an unsure conclusion. Was Lucinda's death the wrath of God, cutting the girl down for her wicked ways? Or was it all meant to be; perhaps, Lucinda should count herself lucky that she found some happiness in the world, even if it was for just a brief moment? Winnie settled on the later.

****

Now is when Jolene enters our story. They assigned her to be Winnie's new roommate. At first, Winnie was cordial toward Jolene, yet, kept aloof in most matters. Hurt can never touch you, if you let no one in.

However, in time, closeness formed between the two. Witnessing Jolene's genuine naïve way, Winnie began to feel responsible for Jolene, taking her under her wing, so to speak.

It was for this reason; Winnie decided one night to set her newfound sister aright, pointing her in the right direction, just as Lucinda did for her. Sitting on the edge of her bed, across the darkness of their room, Winnie gave her well-planned speech to Jolene.

It was not much different from the talk Lucinda gave her, so many months ago. To Winnie's surprise, Jolene wasn't buying any of it.

She couldn't understand it. Why would Jolene turn down the chance of a lifetime? What made matters worse, Jolene had a good counter for every idea Winnie put forth. It was useless. In the end, they agreed to disagree. Still, Jolene's words left a mark on

Winnie. From that day on, the voices of the two philosophies, that of Lucinda and that of Jolene, would echo, arguing in her mind. Which one was right? Winnie knew that someday in her life she would have to decide…just not today.

****

Finally, the day came, Winnie's graduation, Madame sold her to a wealthy Southern gentleman, which was all they told her. She and Jolene would probably never see each other again. A sad fact, neither one of them wanted to address. Such is life.

On the eve of her departure, Winnie lie awake in her bed, anticipation running through her veins. It was then fate took another turn. Jolene whispered across to her.

It was a confession followed by a plea for help. Jolene admitted trying to escape. Using a dining room chair, she tried to scale the wall that surrounded the school. The wall in the garden in the back of the building was never guarded. There was no reason. After all, no one could scale the wall – alone, that is.

"I almost made it to the ledge," Jolene declared. "If you were to help me, I know I could make it over the wall."

"Are you insane?" Winnie growled. "On the eve of my leaving, when all my dreams are about to come true, you ask this of me. If we're caught, I'll lose everything I've hoped and worked for. Not to mention, they'll probably kill us."

"You have to help me, Winnie. You're all I have in this world. When you're gone, I'll be alone. They'll be no one to help me. You're my only hope."

Lucinda's voice echoed in Winnie's mind, reminding and warning her that any other thought or action that does not profit you is against your nature and is a sin. However, there was another voice echoing a completely opposite proposal; it resounded in her heart.

So, despite her newfound philosophy, Winnie agreed to help Jolene escape.

In the garden, each begged the other to give up what they thought of as nonsense. Jolene pleaded Winnie to escape with her. Winnie beseeched Jolene to return to their bedroom. Again, they agreed to disagree.

With the use of one of the dining room chairs, Winnie stood on the chair with her back to the wall. With a quick boost, she hoisted Jolene over the wall.

Winnie returned to her room, while Jolene ran off into the night. Neither one of them knew what the future held for them, only that they both believed they would never see each other again.

****

We can only imagine how difficult Jolene's life became after their parting. Still, she remained true to her beliefs, holding steadfast. Her life was one hardship after another. One would think Winnie having a completely different outlook would have a different outcome. Their values and viewpoint were poles apart. Shouldn't the results be as diverse?

If you were to use their paths as a gauge to which course is the best, you'd end in confusion, at least by the affect. Do not look for an answer here; there is none.

****

As for Winnie's adventures, it would be more fitting to title them misadventures. It came as a surprise to her. She foresaw only triumph, never defeat, let alone doom and gloom. Oh, she was a survivor, always finding the strength to move forward. Except, heartbreak was something she would never be able to shake off, and there was much to come her way.

Her entire life flew into the opposite direction, a mirror image of the way she pictured it would be. The riches she dreamed for, poverty replaced them. The loves of her life, some proved false, others taken away by death, her youthful health stolen. The unfairness of life is a hard fact to learn and a difficult pill to swallow.

Finally, she reached bottom. She had no money, no home, no family or friends. She walked the streets of New Orleans, sick with the cholera. When she collapsed in the gutter, unconscious, at death's door, an angel came to her rescue.

****

Jonathan Gibbs came from a wealthy family, all of them now passed on, leaving him the Gibbs' fortune and one of the largest mansions in the most affluent part of town.

As a young man, he wanted to follow in his father's footsteps. He spent years at university studying law, followed by years as a lawyer. In time, he not only did as well as his father, he did one better by becoming City Judge. Sadly, this happened after both his parents' passing, too late to rejoice in their pride.

Jonathan was mature looking with graying sides to his dark hair. He could easily be described as handsome, to put it mildly. However the features that made him stand out were his intelligence, gentle manner, with an open and giving heart.

His motives were twofold. When Jonathan saw Winnie lying helpless in the street his heart went out to her. When he beheld her beauty, only his heart did the talking.

He took her into his home where she could convalesce. She had her own room, and cared for by the house staff. Jonathan visited her each day, showing his concern and interest, still always being respectful, keeping his distance.

For this reason, she mistrusted him more than any man she ever met, more than any liar or thief. She had become jaded. She could not believe anyone, be it man or woman, could do such an act of compassion without having an ulterior motive.

Kindheartedness is a seed that must be planted deep, watered daily, and nurtured like a small child. Its roots go bottomless. In time it grows thick, tall, and strong. The leaves thick and lush; they are called caring. The blossoms are large and fragrant; they are called sweetness. And the fruit ripens luscious; it is called love.

Without warning or foresight, a day came when Winnie saw with new eyes. First, she saw Jonathan for what he truly was, a loving and caring man – a good man. And in that moment she saw the world, not as it truly was, she saw it as it could be, if you allow it to be.

Falling in love with Jonathan was as easy and as natural as breathing. The more of herself she gave the more she received. He mirrored the love back to her.

In time, without words, both understood they would marry. However, it was the moment Winnie feared the most. There was more to the story, and Jonathan deserved to hear it.

"Jonathan, we need to talk," she said softly.

He laughed slightly. "I thought that's what we were doing."

"No really, we need to talk."

Jonathan went solemn. He knew what she meant.

"Jonathan, you know how grateful I am to you. You've been so good to me. No one has ever been good to me. Which is why I was so suspicious of you, at first, now that I know you better, I know I was wrong. Please, forgive me."

"Winnie, there's nothing to forgive."

Winnie patted the empty space next to her on the divan. "Jonathan, please sit next to me."

When he sat next to her, she took hold of his hand. He looked surprised for a moment, then he looked at their hands, and then up at her face, and smiled.

"I have two things to tell you," she whispered. "I don't know which one to tell you first. They are both key to what I want you to know. So, I'll just say them."

There was a moment of silence, as their eyes met.

"I love you," she announced gently.

"Winnie…!" he said, tightening his grip on her hand.

"No…let me finish, there's more."

A questioning look appeared on his face. Inwardly, Winnie searched for just the right words. Finally, she decided to come to the point, and blurt it out.

"I'm colored."

He stared at her for what seemed like an overly long time, and then he burst into laughter. "What kind of joke is this?"

"I'm serious. I know my skin is light. I've been able to pass for white nearly all my life. But I'm colored! My mother, my father, my whole family is black."

"You're serious," he said as the laughter stopped and the smile left his face.

"I'm dead serious," she released her hand from his grip.

Jonathan spoke not a word, only staring at her. His silence spoke volumes, telling her it was over before it began.

"Don't worry," she said, "I understand the position this puts you in. I'd never hold it against you. I love you too much." She rose from the divan, and then walked toward the door. "I'll be gone in the morning. Thank you, for everything."

Just as her hand touched the doorknob, his hand took hold of her. He spun her around, surrounding her in his strong arms. Pulling her in close, he pressed his lips hard against hers, kissing her.

The world revolved around them, her mind spinning even faster. When he pulled away, her knees went weak. She fell into him, her head flat against his chest, as she tried to catch her breath.

"Don't ever leave me," his voice hummed in her ear. "I love you. From now on, we will face everything, together."

She shook in his arms, crying so hard and long till his shirt was soaked.

****

Winnie agreed to marry Jonathan on one condition and one condition only. She made him swear never to reveal to anyone her true heritage. This was not out of shame, rather out of caring. She understood what such information would do to his career. Jonathan would have proclaimed his love for her on the rooftops, only after a long discussion he agreed to her terms.

****

It was a fairytale wedding. Their life together was what they hoped for and more. If asked, they and all around them would say…*and they lived happily ever after.* There is a reason Children's Stories end with this decree. It's because only a person with a limited exposure to this life could ever believe it. Life is hard. Even when everything is going well, it never ceases to be difficult. There's no *ever after* this side of eternity.

****

Every week, time allowing, Winnie would meet Jonathan for lunch at one of the restaurants near City Hall where his office was. One particular day, Winnie showed for their rendezvous far too early. To pass the time, she entered one of the courtrooms in City Hall. She sat in the back, observing as an outsider to the ways of law.

It was an odd and interesting court case. Sitting before the bench was a frail looking, silent black woman. The judge looked down at her as if she were a pestilence. One by one, they called the witnesses; each one pointing fingers at the woman and making testimony, everything from theft to murder. Winnie thought of only two scenarios; this was either the most evil woman that ever lived, or these were all lies.

In the end, they convicted the woman and sentenced her to hanging within the next twenty-four hours. As they guided the shackled women out of the courtroom, back to her jail cell, Winnie caught a glimpse of the woman's face.

A lightning bolt could not have shocked her more. She recognized her immediately. It was Jolene!

Knowing Jolene so well, Winnie did not believe the accusations. She knew Jolene could only be innocent.

All during lunch, she talked of nothing else with Jonathan. Ending with a tearful plea for him to interact, have the verdict overturned and Jolene officially pardoned. He had the power to do so.

Jonathan never denied his wife anything. As well, he trusted her judgment. It would take much on his part; he would do his best.

****

Blindfolded with the noose around her neck, Jolene prayed, waiting for the trapdoor of the gallows to swing out from under her. Just as she was taking what she believed would be her last breath, they removed the noose. She'd received a last second pardon, from whom and why?

Without explanation, they escorted her to a carriage, and then driven to another part of town, and delivered to the front door of a large elegant mansion. The servant directed her to a sitting room.

He was the most elegant white man Jolene ever met. His grooming with his chiseled good-looks was striking. His smile was welcoming and sincere. Still a young man, there was a noticeable amount of salt and pepper in his hair.

He remained standing, only taking his seat once Jolene did.

"I'm sure you have a thousand questions," he laughed. "My name is Jonathan Gibbs. I'm the City Judge. One of the duties of a City Judge is to oversee the rulings of the Municipal Court. I have the jurisdiction to overturn any of their rulings, which I've done in your favor."

"Why would you do that?" Jolene asked.

"Because I believe you are innocent."

"Why would you think that?"

"Actually, it wasn't me, it was my wife. She watched your trial. She believes you are not guilty. She's a good judge of such things. I trust her. Ah, here is my wife, now," Jonathan announced.

Jolene turned to see a woman as elegant as her husband. Her dark hair done up like a crown, every hair in place. She dressed in a gown made for a princess. Her bare shoulders set off the diamond necklace around her neck. Diamonds sparkled from nearly every finger.

So many years had passed; so much water under the bridge. Jolene did not recognize Winnie. All she saw was a beautiful woman, dressed in a gown fit for royalty.

Winnie reached out, taking Jolene's hand.

"Has it been that long?" Don't you recognize your sister?"

Jolene leaned forward, searching her face.

"Winnie!" Jolene cried.

"Yes, but no longer just Winnie. I'm now Mrs. Gibbs," Winnie smiled at Jonathan. "I've worried everyday since the night I helped you over the wall of Madame Charbonneau's school. You were the sister I never had. I'm sorry for all you've gone through. If only I'd been there. All that will change from now on." Winnie turned to Jonathan "Can she stay with us?"

"Of course, if it makes you happy," Jonathan replied with a smile.

"Yes, it would!" Winnie said, rising to her feet. Still holding Jolene's hand, she pulled her up.

"Oh, my dear sister…" Winnie cried. The two women hugged, holding each other, in tears.

****

Some like to use the word luck, others say there is no such thing, that we make our own destiny. And still others believe we are in the hands of God. Who can explain?

Life in the Gibbs home became good, knowing happiness with no bounds. Both Winnie and Jolene traveled a long road of sorrow to get to a place of contentment.

True sisters they were, together, with Jonathan, they were now a family.

"If ever I'm a hindrance..." Jolene remarked to Winnie, as the two women looked out of the library window at the rainstorm whirling outside.

"Nonsense," Winnie declared. "Jonathan has grown to love you nearly as much as I do. You are my sister, from now until forever."

"But, if...?" Jolene continued.

"No ifs, ands, or buts, my dear," Winnie said, the two holding hands admiring the storm outside. "You are my sister; and right now, I'm going to need you more than ever."

"How is that? Jolene asked.

Winnie turned away from the storm, smiling at Jolene. "I haven't said anything to Jonathan, yet. So, don't say a word, but, you are going to be an aunt."

Six

The Little Red Haired Girl

The Gibbs home was a happy one. Despite living with many secrets, and as all of us know secrets lead to lies, and lies lead to living a life in a manner other than what is natural.

Winnie and Jonathan held a secret. A happy married couple loved and envied by the upper-crust of New Orleans society. They moved about through the public as the darlings of the city.

When they married, Winnie made Jonathan swear to secrecy to never reveal her true bloodline. As light skinned as she was, she was a black woman, third generation African.

If you knew Winnie, you'd know she was a woman who would be proud of whom she was, and would scream her heritage to the world from the rooftop. However, if you knew how much she loved her husband, Jonathan, you would not hold it against her.

All would be lost if even a rumor started. Jonathan's life would be in ruin, their marriage, and now the future of their child growing within her.

Jolene held a secret, also. Both she and Winnie were sisters in spirit. They treated Jolene like a true part of the family. However, when strangers were around, she played the part of one of the house staff, which in itself wasn't too difficult for Jolene. Although it tormented Winnie to see Jolene lowered in her presence, even though Jolene was never the sort to complain.

Every day Jolene spent hours in the kitchen alongside Ma Cherie, the cook. Ma Cherie was an older black woman with a strong sense of self-worth, knowledge of cooking and of the Bible. Jolene adored Ma Cherie; as well the work filled her days with a feeling of usefulness.

There is an edict in the universe that all that is secret will become known eventually. Unknown to them, the peace that draped the Gibb household would someday be lifted, their lives overturned.

That turning point started the night Winnie announced she was with child. Just after dinner, all three of them, Jolene, Winnie and Jonathan were in the sitting room. Jolene knew Winnie was going to tell Jonathan. She expressed that they should be alone for such a moment, however Winnie insisted that she be present.

"You're having what…?" Jonathan shouted, jumping to his feet. He was beside himself, not knowing what to do first. Finally, he took Winnie up in his arms, kissing her.

Jolene stood off to the side, applauding.

"When….when…?" Jonathan asked.

"…eight months."

"I don't think he can wait that long," Jolene laughed.

It was true; he felt excited and overjoyed, doing what most men do, he mollycoddled his wife, as if she were made of cotton.

"I'm not going to break," Winnie expressed with amusement.

"Is it a boy or a girl?" he asked.

"Now, how would I know," Winnie laughed; Jolene joined in. "I hope it's a boy, and he looks like you," Winnie added.

"Well, I hope it's a girl and she looks just like you," he countered with delight.

That was when the smile left Winnie's face. Jonathan was too elated to notice. However, Jolene noticed.

****

A few days later in the afternoon while Jonathan was away at work, Winnie and Jolene sat in the sitting room, warming up to a cozy fire. Jolene noticed the change that recently come over Winnie, the blank stare of someone in deep thought, fearing what may come next and looking for a solution. Winnie sat across from Jolene, staring into the flames.

"Winnie…?"

"Hmm…?"

"Winnie, look at me?"

She raised her head slowly as if it weighed a ton, her face vacant with her eyes empty of any emotion.

"Winnie, what is wrong? I know you. Something's wrong. This should be the happiest time of your life. You have a husband who loves you, a fine home, not to mention you're receiving the blessing of a child. What is wrong?"

Winnie's expression changed, her eyes became clear and intense. Leaning forward, she spoke low and softly, as if no one except Jolene should hear.

"When I was little, living on the plantation, there was one particular overseer that I remember well. I don't remember his name. There was little to remember him by. I just remember he was a tall, lanky, dark haired white man. He had the strangest way of talking. He spoke in a manner I never heard before. I found out he was Irish, it was his thick Irish brogue that set him off from all the others. You see, it was the way his folks raised him that gave him the strong accent even though he was born here. It was his parents that were born in Ireland.

"He was married. He and his wife lived on the plantation. She was a tall, thin white woman with long black hair. They had two small boys, both their hair was as dark and wavy as their parents'.

"A year or so later, they had another child. I watched the woman from afar, her belly getting bigger every month till she looked ready to burst. I wondered what the baby would be, another boy, or finally a daughter with dark hair and fair skin like her mother.

"This time it was a girl. Over the years, I watched her grow. When she was older, I'd see her playing with her brothers. There was something different about this little girl. She didn't look anything like her two brothers, nor did she look like her parents. Strangest thing...her hair was red, like a head full of fire, it was.

"I didn't understand, so I asked my mother about this. She said, 'It's because she's Irish. Many Irish folk have bright red hair.' I still didn't understand. If the whole family had dark-hair, why did she have red hair? 'Because somebody in her family, a grandparent maybe, had red hair', my mother tried to explain. 'Things like that sometimes skip a generation, and then just pop up when you least expect it. Just look at you, ya got light skin, not like me or your daddy. Probably, somewhere down the line, one of your great grand folk had light skin, and it just popped up again with you. Things like that happen all the time'."

"I don't understand what you're getting at?" Jolene whispered, shaking her head in confusion.

"Don't you see, Jolene? I'm just like the little red haired girl. All my family, as far back as I can remember, were of dark black skin. Yet, look at me, how light my skin is. Somewhere in my lineage, a long time ago, there was someone as light or even white. That was lost in my family tree, skipping generation after generation. Then suddenly, I popped up, white as a cloud.

"Jonathan is white from a white family; I'm light from a black family. What will our child be? Will he look like him, like me, or like Jonathan's father or mother, or perhaps, his grandparents? It's possible. It's also possible, he'll look like my folks, or my grandparents from Africa. What if my baby is black?"

"Then you'll love him with all your heart!" Jolene stated sternly, nearly shouting. "Your child will be a combination of all you are and all Jonathan is. It will be a testimony to the love you share for each other," Jolene added.

"And what will happen to Jonathan? Having a black mistress may be frowned on, but accepted. Having a black bastard child is accepted also. Except having a black wife and a black child is enough for the world to turn its back on him. He will lose everything, his career, his wealth, everything," Winnie argued.

"So you lose everything?" Jolene disputed. "Even then you will have more than most folks."

"Like what?"

"You'll have your life, your health, your family, you'll have love. Winnie, don't you understand? I'm grateful for my life with you and Jonathan, except I'd give it all away for what you have, a man that loves you, and now a baby to love. Have some faith. Somehow, you'll get by."

Winnie shook her head. "No, I can't do that to Jonathan."

"How do you know?" Jolene continued. "Speak to him, see how he feels."

"No!" Winnie insisted, "And don't you ever mention this to Jonathan." A strange look washed over Winnie's face. "If the child is black, we need to have an alternate plan."

Jolene could only speculate what that plan might be.

****

Days passed with neither Jolene nor Winnie speaking of the matter. In fact, it was uncomfortable the way they both skirted the issue. Jolene felt tempted to mention it, however, afraid she might learn Winnie's alternate plan. There were ways a woman could end a pregnancy, all of them dangerous. If that's what Winnie was thinking of as an alternate plan, Jolene would be against it. Loving friend and sister or not, Jolene knew she would have to stand up to Winnie.

What was distressing was Jolene had no one to confide in, certainly not Jonathan. She felt tempted to speak with Ma Cherie. The sweet old woman with a heart of gold would know what to do. Except she'd made a promise to Winnie never to say a word to anyone, and Jolene was the sort to keep a promise. To speak in confidence of the matter, even in the secrecy of the kitchen, the domain of Ma Cherie, to let the cat out of the bag, might mean more trouble. Besides, you can't come to an answer till you know the question.

****

It was at the time when Winnie was beginning to show, her belly slowly growing larger into a dome holding her child, her face a little rounder with a healthy glow. One of the house staff came up to her bedroom to summon her to the sitting room where her husband waited.

This was strange, as it was midafternoon; Jonathan never came home so early. When she entered the sitting room, Jonathan stood, facing her with the largest smile. Standing next to him was a frail, thin, elderly, white man, dressed in an elegant dark suit. The man was old enough to be Jonathan's grandfather with a full head of silver hair that matched his bushy mustache, covering so much of his mouth it took a moment for Winnie to realize he was smiling.

"Come in, darling," Jonathan called, reaching out to her. "There's someone I'd like for you to meet." When she stood before them, the old man reached out, taking her hand, he kissed it. "This is Dr. Jean de Malades. He's been our family doctor since before I was born."

"In fact, I brought this young man into the world," Dr. de Malades added, smiling at Jonathan and then at Winnie.

Jonathan continued, "I trust the good doctor, fully. I told him about your condition, he's agreed to take your case."

"Case…? You're still thinking in legal terms, my boy," Laughed the old man. Still holding her hand, he smiled into Winnie's eyes. "I can see you weren't prepared for this, my child," the doctor said in a kind and gentle manner. "Taking care of your baby doesn't start at birth, it starts now. Early care and guidance will insure an easier delivery, which means good health for mother and child." The old man's smile grew larger. "Don't look so down, it's not as bad as it sounds. I'll visit you once each week, checking how you're coming along, how you're sleeping, eating, giving you regular checkups."

"Who will do the delivery?" Winnie asked.

"I will, of course."

Winnie didn't look too pleased. "I was hoping to use a midwife."

"I'll have a midwife to help me. Don't worry you'll be in good hands."

Winnie looked to Jonathan. He was smiling from ear to ear, clearly pleased with himself. She didn't want to disappoint him. Then she looked at the doctor. He seemed harmless enough.

What worried her was what can a doctor deduce from an examination? Could he identify her true lineage? What if the child was black, could he be expected to keep it to himself, or would all of New Orleans know of it by the next morning? Winnie could think of no way out of the situation, perhaps, at a later time, only, not today.

Winnie consented, "Very well, doctor, how and when do we start?"

A look of relief glowed on Jonathan's face.

"We can start right now, right here, starting with a full examination," de Malades said, and then turned to Jonathan, "Jonathan, my boy, why don't you leave us for a few minutes? I'll call you when we're finished."

"Dr. de Malades, don't take this wrong," Winnie said, "I'd feel more comfortable if there was another woman in the room."

"Don't apologize, my dear. I understand, completely," said de Malades.

Winnie looked to Jonathan. "Dear, would you ask Jolene to step in for a moment, please?"

"Of course," he said, leaving the room.

A minute later, Jolene entered.

"Lock the door," the doctor told Jolene. "I'm going to examine your mistress; I'll need your help." He asked this in a kindly manner, nevertheless, it was clear he believed Jolene to be one of the house staff.

After locking the door, Jolene remained silent, standing ready for instruction.

Dr. de Malades opened his small black satchel, taking out a stethoscope.

"You need to remove your dress. You can leave on your undergarments," he announced, matter-of-factly.

Jolene helped Winnie undress.

To Winnie's surprise, the examination wasn't nearly as uncomfortable as she feared. Years of experience gave de Malades a bedside manner superior to other doctors half his age.

Still, the procedure left Winnie unsure. She questioned the doctor, as she dressed with Jolene's help.

"So, doctor, what are your findings?"

"I'd say you're going to have a baby," he said jokingly.

"No, doctor, I'm serious. Please, tell me."

"You're young and healthy; I can see no reason for you to worry. I predict a healthy baby."

"What else can you tell me?" Winnie continued to probe.

"What more can I say. All is well."

Winnie stammered her words. "I mean, can you tell anything about the child. Will it be a boy or girl?"

Dr. de Malades laughed; holding up his stethoscope to her. "Madame, this is not a crystal ball," he said before returning it to his satchel. He smiled at her. "However, in my years of experience, I feel comfortable saying that by the way the child is sitting up so high; I'd venture to say it's a boy."

"One thing else…" Winnie added.

He looked at her, waiting.

"My grandfather had a weak heart. He died young because of it. I've heard of such things skipping generations and then turning up generations later. Is that true, doctor?"

He shook his head, laughing. "You young first-time mothers are all alike. Where do you get such notions?"

"But it is possible, doctor?"

"I repeat: you're young, healthy, as is your husband. I see no reason to worry. That is my first order of the day. Stop worrying."

Taking up his bag, he handed Winnie his card.

"This is my address. Don't hesitate to reach out to me, for any reason. I'll see you in a week's time." He started for the door. "Don't worry, I can show myself out." He told Jolene. "Now, you take good care of your mistress, you hear?"

Seven

Spewing Evil

If you do something long enough, in time it becomes habit. Dr. de Malades' weekly visits became commonplace. In fact, everyone's life in the Gibbs' manor became routine. Jonathan spent his days at work, returning in the evenings, doting on his wife. Jolene kept Winnie company, as her best and closes friend. When she wasn't at Winnie's side, she was in the kitchen with Ma Cherie cooking and baking.

Winnie, she seemed happy enough, keeping her concerns hidden from the world. All the while the child in her grew, as did she, till she was a round, puffy, little creation, always in some form of discomfort.

It wasn't only Winnie who had concerns. Jolene battled within her soul if she should confide her distress concerning Winnie's beliefs with Ma Cherie. Knowing the older woman's heart with years of wisdom, Jolene told her what Winnie said, also expressing her fears for her friend and the child.

Ma Cherie's advice was this: Prayer becomes necessary, above all else as is always the case, and to not mention a word of anything to anyone about the matter. It was all up to Winnie. The next card was hers to play. Only then would they be able to have a say. For now, let sleeping dogs lie.

Once again, Ma Cherie's good judgment proved to be the right way to go. In time, Winnie came around to speaking of the matter with both of them. It was late in the afternoon in the study with Jonathan at work. Winnie laid out her plan to the only two people in the world she could trust, excluding Jonathan. What she proposed was far more elaborate, nothing quite what they expected.

"I want you both to swear that whatever I tell you will never leave this room," Winnie pleaded.

The two women nodded agreeing. Winnie continued.

"Don't say a word until I've finished what I have to say. I'm not insane. I've thought about this for a long time.

"In a few weeks my child will be here. As you both know, there is a chance my baby will be black. Only we three know that. If so, I see nothing other than ruin. So, I've come up with a plan.

"I've bought a small cottage just a few miles from the edge of the city, an hour's carriage drive." She turned to Jolene. "I want you to move into that cottage. We'll tell Jonathan you've left to stay with family."

Winnie Looked at Ma Cherie. "When the time comes for the child's birth, we won't send for Dr. de Malades; we'll do the delivery ourselves. I know you have midwife knowledge."

Winnie continued in a whisper. "If the child turns out light-skinned, there is no issue." Again, she looked to Jolene. "Then I will call you back. I'll tell Jonathan it didn't work out with your family. He will welcome you back, I just know it."

"What if the child...what if the child is black?" Jolene asked, hesitantly.

"Then, Ma Cherie will bring the child to live with you. I'll visit whenever I can. In time, you can return. We'll tell everyone the child is yours."

Ma Cherie interrupted, "And what will you tell your husband, when there is no child? What about Dr. de Malades? For that matter, what will you tell the world about this missing child?"

Winnie had an answer prepared. "As for Dr. de Malades, we tell him it all happened so fast; we didn't have time to call for him. As for Jonathan and the rest of the world, the child was stillborn."

"What about the body?" Jolene asked coldly.

"Jonathan is sure to be waiting in the sitting room. I'll tell him I didn't want him to go through heartbreak; so, I had the body taken down the rear stairs and buried in our back garden. Don't you worry, Jonathan will believe me. Of course, Ma Cherie, you will go down the rear stairs, only, to take the child to Jolene."

Winnie sat before them, looking to her friends, a questioning look on her face. Jolene and Ma Cherie stared at her, dumbfounded.

"Winnie, you are my best friend," Jolene said. "I can't think of anything I wouldn't do for you. But this..." Jolene went silent, looking down at her hands, not wanting to look eye to eye with Winnie.

Winnie turned to Ma Cherie, hoping for some words of encouragement.

"Winnie...dear child...I stood next to you in church the day you turned your back on your old life. My heart was so full. I love you, child. You just told us you're not insane. I actually wish you were. I'd feel better if you were. Can't you hear the evil that's spewing from your mouth? It's wrong in so many ways.

"You have a husband who loves you; he would never leave you, no matter what. At your wedding you made a vow to God. You're turning your back on both your husband

and God. You're asking your two closest friends to lie for you. Then there's the child, you're willing to turn your back on your own child over their skin color. Don't forget your own dignity, what becomes of that? And lastly, your race, to deny it, to be ashamed of it, to turn you back on it is a sad affair. No, everything you're proposing is wrong, very wrong, and moreover very selfish. I'll have nothing to do with it."

Winnie turned to Jolene. "Do you feel the same?"

Jolene looked directly at Winnie, nodding her head that she did feel the same.

"Very well," Winnie said, "If that's the way you feel. But understand this is what I'm going to do, with or without your help. If I don't, consider this, Jonathan will lose his job and standing in the community. In time, he will lose everything, his wealthy, this house, everything." She addressed Jolene first. "At that point you will be back on the streets, once more, with no home, no money and no hope." Then she spoke to Ma Cherie. "They'll sell you as a cook, hopefully, not as a laborer to some plantation."

Jolene and Ma Cherie quietly listened.

"As for my marriage, where would we go, once the world knows the truth? Only a life in the wilderness would be possible, even then there will be great danger. And as for my child, the best for him will be a life of hard labor, or worse.

"You say I'm acting in the wrong, well then, tell me what's right? You say I'm acting selfish, but it's not just me I'm thinking of. It's all of us. Our entire world will be ruined. I'd rather lie to my husband than see him destroyed. I'd rather scheme then see my two loved ones sold into slaver or starving in the streets. And lastly, I would sooner lose my child's love then have his future shattered with nothing to look to other than the sweat of his brow, belittled, and mistreated. So, if either of you cannot think of a better way, we will continue with my plan."

Jolene and Ma Cherie sat silently staring at Winnie. Finally, Ma Cherie broke the stillness.

"Very well, I will do it, only not for any of the reasons you have said. I still think you are wrong. Although there was something you said at the beginning, which made me want to help you. You said that if we refused to help, you would still go with your plan. So, I will be a part of it, in hopes that I might see that few, if anyone, gets hurt."

The look on Jolene's face told it all, she felt the same as Ma Cherie, agreeing to being a part of it, against her better judgment.

Like three ghosts, without a sound, they rose, leaving the room. It would be a week before they spoke of it again.

Eight

Lonesome

They started off early in the morning, just after Jonathan left for work. They went by hired carriage, the back of which they filled with food and supplies. The cabbie thought it nothing more than a slave girl traveling with her white mistress. Noticing the woman was pregnant, he did his best to avoid bumps and dips in the road.

It was a quaint, one-story cottage, whitewashed walls outside and within with a thatched roof. A low picket fence surrounded the half-acre property, a path from the gate to the front door with flowers on both sides of the walkway and a small garden in front of the home. It was more than just livable, it was charming. In every direction was a stunning view of fields with green forests of large trees beyond.

The cabbie carted all the food and supplies into the small kitchen, and then he returned to the carriage to wait.

Off the kitchen was a living area, beyond that were two bedrooms. Winnie thought of everything. The home was completely well furnished. Jolene would want for nothing.

They spoke softly with each other, as they looked out the back window. The backyard was small with acres of field beyond the fence, and tall wood passed that.

"You see the church steeple beyond those trees," Winnie said, pointing passed the fields to the north. "There's a small community there, mostly folks who work in the city and the harbors. There are a few shops there, if you need anything. Only, please don't visit it, yet. If we have to carry out the plan, it would look strange for a woman who is not pregnant to show up the next week with a newborn. So, try to stay to yourself. Don't worry, I will send you whatever you need each week by carriage. We can communicate by letter."

Winnie could not ignore the sadness that swept across Jolene's face. She was asking much of her, and she knew it.

"I don't know how to ever thank you," Winnie moaned, reaching out, taking hold of Jolene by the hand.

"It's all right," Jolene replied, looking Winnie squarely in the eye. "If you can't ask your sister, who can you ask?"

Stepping outside, silently, the two women hugged good-bye. The cabbie helped Winnie up into the carriage. As they pulled away, Winnie turned, continuing to wave good-bye. Jolene stood at the front gate till the carriage disappeared over the horizon.

Many times, Jolene had gone through much hardship, always on her own. However, at that moment she never felt that alone in her life.

****

Jonathan placed his knife and fork down, looking up at Winnie. "I don't understand," he questioned, sounding disappointed. "Why would she just get up and leave like that? Wasn't she happy living here?"

"Of course she was, darling. It's like I said she got a letter from some family members who are now free. They've invited her to live with them. She knows we love her, except now she has a real family…her family."

"…Where?" he asked bluntly.

"Ah…Mississippi," Winnie blurted out off the top of her head.

"Mississippi?" he echoed. "How is she going to get all the way to Mississippi, on her own?"

"By train," Winnie answered. "I hope you don't mind, I gave her some money?"

"Of course, I don't, only, it doesn't make sense. I go to work in the morning, I come home in the evening, and she's gone without a word of good-bye."

"She was just so excited about being with her real family."

Jonathan took up his knife and fork, again. "Well, I think it's a shame. She would have made such a wonderful aunt for little William."

Now, Winnie placed her knife and fork down. "And who is little William?"

"Our son," he replies, as if it were common knowledge.

"And how do you know I'm having a boy?"

"I can feel it in my bones," he smiled.

"…a gut feeling?" Winnie smirked.

"Something like that."

"What about the name William?"

"It was my father's name. I just thought I'd run it by you to see how it sounded."

"Sounds all right, as names go. So, tell me is there anything else you feel in your gut that I need to know?"

He smiled, reaching out, taking her hand. "Only that I love you."

****

It was all so confusing for Jolene. She'd been through so much in her life, all of it with no one at her side. Then why now did she feel so alone, a loneliness that went straight to the bone? Perhaps, it was because she never had anyplace or anyone to miss. She never was as happy in her entire life as she was living with Winnie and Jonathan.

She couldn't sleep a wink that first night. Lighting a fire, she pulled up a chair, staring into the flames till it turned to red embers, and finally went cold, turning to ashes. Then she moved the chair to the back window overlooking the field with the full moon lighting up the world.

She remembered when she was young that folks told her never to stare at the moon; you'd go mad. Jolene gazed straight into the moon, like it was the love of her life, never blinking. If it made her go mad, so be it.

So slowly that it was difficult to notice, the moon moved across the sky, sinking into the edge of the world as the sun peered over the horizon. It was her first day, already it was unbearable.

She began to feel sleepy, nevertheless, she knew she needed to keep busy and stay awake till that night. If she didn't, she'd wake in the night, wide awake, only to fall asleep in the daytime. She knew better than to let that happen. Her life was turned around enough.

****

A week passed, a hired carriage made the first delivery to Jolene. It was more than enough to eat for a month, let alone a week. Mixed with the supplies was a letter from Winnie.

My dearest sister,

All is well here; I hope it is the same with you. Jonathan was disappointed to hear you left and I miss you so.

If you need anything, send a letter back with the cabbie.

All my love,

Winnie

To Jolene's dismay, it was just a short poorly composed update of what was going on in the Gibbs' household. Not enough to quench Jolene's inquisitiveness, and did not come close to extinguishing the flames of her lonesomeness brought on by such seclusion.

Within the envelope was a good amount of money. There was a P.S. to the letter instructing to buy goats, good milking goats. That way, if she were to house the child, there would be no need for a wet nurse.

She clearly remembered Winnie's warning about going to the nearby town, and the consequences of someone seeing her without child, and then possibly with a newborn only a few weeks later. Still the isolation became too much to put up with. Just to hear another human voice other than her own muffled in her mind would make all the difference between feeling like a human being again and going mad.

****

In the early morning, she left the house, walked across the field toward the church steeple off in the distance.

Jolene remained in the woods, observing the town from afar. The town was already buzzing with activity. Shops were beginning to open, children gathered in front of the schoolhouse, folks young and old, black and white, going from here to there, caught in the hustle and bustle of their lives.

"Planning on robbing the bank?" a deep, husky voice whispered behind her. Jolene jumped into the air, spinning around. A black man stood before her, smiling. "I'm afraid you're out of luck," he continued, "We don't have one," he laughed.

His smile was comforting, she immediately felt at ease.

"I didn't know you were there. You nearly scared the life out of me," she said.

"Sorry. I like to walk in the forest for my morning prayers."

That was when Jolene noticed he wore a white clerical collar.

"Oh, you're a reverend? Is that your church?" she asked, pointing to the high steeple.

The statement caused him to burst into thunderous laughter. "I wish! No, that's the white church. You see that barn at the end of the street? That's the black church; that's my church."

"What town is this?" she asked.

"They call it Sans Nom. It's just a small community of folks that work at the local farms and plantations, mostly whites, a few blacks, some even are free. Seems many of the plantation owners believe religion keeps a slave in line. That's why they gave me the barn to use as a church in the first place. Don't look like that; we cleaned it out real good before we moved in." He shook his head. "Forgive me; I haven't even introduced myself. I'm the Reverend Philip Anderson. The barn is not only our church; it's where I live with my sister, Celene. And you are...?"

"Jolene Fairchild," she replied, the two shook hands.

It was then Jolene took full notice of his appearance.

Reverend Philip Anderson was a large man with a winning smile with dark piercing eyes. He was tall, hefty, and handsome, his close-cropped hair and beard framed his attractive face. He was clearly older than Jolene, yet not by more than six or seven year.

"Are you just passing through?" he asked.

Jolene turned, pointing in the direction from where she came. "No, I live a slight ways that way, the whitewashed house with the thatched roof. My mistress bought it for a get-away home where she could be alone."

"She lives with you?"

"Oh, no, she seldom comes. I live alone."

"Alone, in the middle of a field, a beautiful woman living alone…?"

The question made her unnerved, although inwardly it pleased her.

He continued, "Well, we can soon fix that. Come to our church this Sunday. I'll introduce you to the congregation."

"That sounds nice," Jolene replied, sounding a bit put off by the offer. It was then she realized she was in too deep. She needed to back away, and leave. "I do have to get back. It was very nice meeting you," she said backing away slowly, turning, and walking away.

"Don't forget this Sunday!" he shouted off to her.

****

Sunday came, Jolene felt tempted to take up Philip's invitation, and go to the church in Sans Nom. Still, she knew it was best not to. It was bad enough someone now knew she lived alone and childless.

The urge to go was so strong, it made the loneliness deeper, making the hours past slower, making the day immeasurable.

As the sun was setting, she looked out the back window. She could see the figure of someone off in the distance, walking through the field, toward the house. She suspected it was the Reverend coming to check on her, wondering why she hadn't attended church service. However, as the person approached, she realized it was a woman.

She opened the back window, as the woman came nearer. She was a lovely black woman, slender, young, wearing a familiar smile. A wicker basket hung from her arm.

"You must be Jolene," the woman called out.

"Yes, how did you know?" Jolene asked as the woman stepped up to the window.

"My name's Celene, Philip's my brother. He mentioned you to me."

"He spoke of you, too," Jolene responded. "Would you like to come in?"

"That's all right, I need to get back before it get's too late. I just wanted to welcome you to the area. Oh, yeah, here's a little something I brought for you."

She handed Jolene the basket. Jolene peered within. It was two loaves of homemade bread.

"Toast it up with some butter, ain't nothin' better."

"Well, that's very kind of you," Jolene said.

"To be honest," Celene continued, "we were expecting you today at church. When you didn't show, we thought it best to see if you were all right. Philip would have come, only he's busy."

There was a nervous moment of silence between the two, which Celene broke.

"I don't know why I said that, it's a little bit of a small lie. Actually, besides comin' here to welcome you, there are other reasons. Not much excites, my brother, Philip, but you sure got to him. He would and should have come himself, except he's the shy type. And the last reason is that I'm just a nosy so-and-so."

Truth is the strongest icebreaker. The two women roared with laughter.

Celene started walking off. "Well, I'd like to stay; only I want to get back before dark."

"Celene, wait! What about your basket?"

She walked a few steps backwards as she spoke. "I guess you'll just have to come to church next Sunday to return it."

Nine

By Their Fruit

"Well, it seems I was wrong," Dr. de Malades admitted. "I was hoping you'd deliver in two weeks, but like everything else, nothing goes as planned."

"So, when am I due?" Winnie asked nervously.

"Remember you must remain calm," he warned as he returned his stethoscope. "I'd say within the next twenty-four hours, maybe forty-eight, no longer."

Since Jolene's departure, Ma Cherie stayed at Winnie's side during her weekly exams by Dr. de Malades. The two women's eyes locked, knowing what was to come.

"I'll always leave word about where I'll be. Send for me, day or night, I'll get here as soon as I can." He looked to Ma Cherie. "I won't bring a midwife. I'm sure Ma Cherie, here, is more than capable."

Ma Cherie helped Winnie with her clothes. The doctor gave one last piece of advice. "Now, don't you worry, you're young and healthy. I've done this hundreds of time. You'll have a fine healthy baby." He smiled at her. "I guess you're excited to tell your husband?"

Again, the eyes of the two women locked. Just the thought of Jonathan caused their bodies to stiffen, putting their nerves on edge.

****

Jonathan looked across the dinner table at Winnie, an unsure expression on his face. "I've got something to tell you," he said shyly.

"I got something to tell you, too," Winnie replied.

Jonathan's face beamed with excitement. He figuring it had something to do with the baby, a topic they talked about often, now more so as the date approached. Winnie hadn't mentioned the earlier date predicted by Dr. de Malades. "What is it?" he asked with enthusiasm.

"No, darling, you were first, so, you go first."

There was a disappointment in Jonathan that he did his best to not show. In fact, he dreaded having to say, what he feared my upset her.

He spoke slowly. "Well…I received a wire from the Governor. He wants us to come to Baton Rouge, to the capital. He says he has plans for me. I think I know what that means. I think he's going to offer me an official position in the capital in Baton Rouge. He'd like us to come for a few days, so he and I can talk things over. I wired him back that I'd have to speak with you, first. Now that I think about it, you shouldn't be traveling in your condition. I'll have to ask him if we can do this at a later date."

"...Nonsense!" Winnie declared, reaching across the table, placing her hand on his. "Strike while the iron is hot. If you don't take advantage of this now, the opportunity may not be there later. You may regret it for the rest of your life. And I don't want to be the reason it doesn't happen."

"What about you, my love?" he asked.

"I'll be fine."

"What about the baby?" he complained. "I don't want to miss the birth of my son."

He still insisted the child would be a boy, fully believing they'd name him William.

"I'm not due for another two weeks," she insisted. "You'll be back before then."

"Are you sure?" he asked, sounding concerned.

"Yes, Dr. de Malades told me so, just today. Don't worry. I won't let you miss the birth of your...son...I promise," she laughed.

Shame poisoned her blood, surging up her spine, flowing into all the fibers of her being. She succeeded in not showing it; still, it ate at her from the inside, like the viper that it was. Lying to her husband, something she had never done before, nor did she believe she ever would. Only, now, here she was lying as if he meant nothing to her, which was not the case. Jonathan was everything to her.

Inwardly, she felt the distance between them grow, a distance she created, and one Jonathan wasn't even aware of.

It was that part of her old self, the one she declared dead and buried, the resurrection of the beast.

"Perhaps, you're right," he admitted. "I'll leave first thing in the morning. This way I'll be back in plenty of time."

They both smiled at each other with approval, one smile was false.

"So, what was it that you wanted to tell me?" he asked.

Still smiling, her mind raced for an answer.

"Oh, I received a letter from Jolene."

"And how is she?"

"She writes she's just fine. The most important part is she says she thinks she met that special someone."

There was a strong element of truth to this statement. Winnie was quoting according to Jolene's recent letter. Winnie added a flare of drama to it, as Jolene never mentioned meeting someone any more than a person of interest.

"Good," Jonathan replied. "If anyone deserves to be happy, it's she."

There is no such thing as one lie, for it always leads to another, and perhaps more. Like a lit fuse, it goes on and on till in the end everything explodes.

****

Another Sunday came. Jolene struggled with the thought of going or not going to the church service. In her mind she heard Winnie's warnings, however her heart told her different. It was so difficult for her. The mind speaks in words, but the heart makes itself known in song, and music drowns out everything.

She carried her solitude like some ancient medieval armor, protecting her, yet, stopping the world from touching her, and she it. It was heavyweight armor, a constant burden, pulling her further down into the muck and mire of depression, turning her lovely cottage into a prison cell.

If she had to take Winnie's child in, how would she explain to be one moment without child, and then with child in the next? Then it dawned on her, a scheme. A close friend, a sister of the heart and soul, died in childbirth. No…that was too much…too strong and sad. Perhaps the mother was alone in the world and too poor to care for a child. She would need time to get back up on her feet, and would call for the child once she was in a better place. So, in an act of mercy, Jolene took the child in. This sounded more reasonable, although, it was still a lie, which bothered Jolene down to the bone and into her soul.

When you plant the seed of falsehood, it will soon take root, and in time grow and blossom more lies. *You will know them by their fruit.*

****

From a distance, she could hear the congregation singing hymns from the barn, growing louder and clearer the closer she came. These were worship songs from her childhood. It warmed her heart just to here them. She was beginning to feel at home.

Placing the basket in the crook of her arm, she used her free hand to open the barn door. As soon as she moved it slightly, a young black man held it open for her.

"Welcome, sister," he shouted over the singing, smiling a welcome.

It was an old barn. They cleaned it well; there was no lingering smell of the original inhabitants. It was sparse, walls and a dirt floor. There were no pews or chairs, everyone stood. Having no piano or organ, they sang a cappella.

The congregation consisted of black folk, mostly families, men and women of all ages, and children. Clearly, they dressed in their Sunday finest; however, it would be honest to say nobody looked very prosperous. These were laborers, sharecroppers, and slaves, people who worked hard everyday...the *Salt of the Earth*.

Jolene felt just fine standing in the back. Someone's hand went up, waving her to come down front. It was Celene, smiling at her. Though she really didn't want to, being a timid one, yet not wanting to be offensive, Jolene went to stand next to her newfound friend.

At the end of the hymn, Reverend Anderson, Philip that is, stood facing them all. No altar, no pulpit, candles or crosses, just a man of God. He smiled at Jolene before he started to speak, she smiled shyly back.

Jolene heard many preachers in her time, except Philip was different. He spoke softly and kindly. From the look on his face, you could tell that he was glad to be there, caring for every one of them. From the looks on their faces, they felt the same about him.

There was no fire and brimstone, only encouragement with a strong emphasis on love. He was knowledgeable, of the Bible and life in general. Never did his winning smile ever leave his face. It was a smile of sincerity.

Jolene couldn't help notice that now and then he'd look directly at her, smiling. She found herself smiling back each time and her bashfulness melting away.

When the service was over, it surprised Jolene that no one went home. They all went outside to the back of the building where there were benches and tables. There they held the grandest of church picnics.

"I'm afraid I didn't bring anything," Jolene apologized.

"Don't ya worry none, sister," said one of the women. "We do this lots of times. You can bring somethin' next time. Here, let me make up a plate for ya."

The generosity of these people moved Jolene's spirit, and the warmth coming from them melted her heart. It was good to once again be among good people.

It was getting late when the picnic broke up; folks started to go to their homes. Though she would never admit it, Jolene felt disappointed she never once got to speak with Philip. Everyone, including some of the children wanted some of his time, and he didn't want to disappoint any of them. When most of the folks had left, Philip came over to sit down next to Jolene.

"Did you have a good time?" he asked.

"Yes I did," she answered, smiling.

"Well, I'm glad you came."

"I'm glad I came, too. Oh, by the way, Reverend, I mean, Philip," she corrected herself when she saw the look of disappointment on Philip's face when she called him 'Reverend'. "I'm looking to have a small herd of goats, good milking goat. Do you know of where I can buy some?"

"I know just the man," Philip answered. "I'll have him contact you."

There was a long moment of painful stillness between them, which Jolene then broke. "I guess I should be getting on home," she announced, rising to her feet.

"It's getting late. Why don't I walk you home?" he asked to her surprise.

"Gee, I don't know."

"If it makes you uncomfortable to be alone with me, then my sister, Celene, could come with us."

"Did I hear my name?" Celene called from across the clearing.

"I was just telling Jolene, you and I could walk her home," he called back.

"My feet are killing me," Celene waved them on. "You two go without me."

"That's all right, Reverend, I'll be fine," Jolene said.

"Philip, call me Philip."

"I'll be fine, Philip," she told him as she started to walk away.

"Jolene?" he said, stopping her. "I'd like to call on you sometime."

She smiled wide to him. "I'd like that."

****

A moment after Jonathan's wire to the Governor, excepting his invitation was off to the capital, so was Jonathan. The wire included his apologies concerning his wife. Because of her condition, she would not be accompanying him.

"You sure you don't mind me going?" Jonathan asked Winnie as their carriage pulled to the train station.

"Of course not, I want you to go. I'm so proud of you. What do you think the Governor wants to discuss with you?" Winnie asked.

He leaned over to her, smiling, he whispered. "Like I said, I suspect a job offering." He looked about to be sure no one was listening. "Now, keep this under your hat. I suspect he may ask me to run for mayor of New Orleans."

A smile of amazement grew across Winnie's face. "You think so? What will you say if he does?"

"If he's willing to back me, of course I will. However, let's not get ahead of ourselves." He stood up in the carriage, bent low, and kissed her, "Stay seated," he whispered. "No need to get up. You can wave me good-bye from here." Stepping out of the carriage, he looked up to her. "Remember, if anything happens, you wire me, and I'll rush home."

"Nothing's going to happen," she assured him. "Dr. de Malades said it won't be for another week and a half. You'll be back before then."

"I love you," were his parting words.

"I love you, too," she called back.

Winnie had the driver position the carriage so she could wave good-bye. Jonathan leaned out one of the windows of his private compartment on the train, smiling and waving back. He continued doing this till the trees after the turn hide the station. From the station, the train disappeared over the horizon.

Ten

He Will Take Care of You

Winnie and Ma Cherie discussed hiring a midwife. Actually, it was more of an argument than a discussion. With the absence of the good doctor, Ma Cherie, though sure of her abilities, felt better if there was another knowledgeable person along. Winnie shot down the idea the second Ma Cherie raised it. She wanted no one other than those already involved to be a part of her plan. Some folk have a wagging tongue, or may use the leverage to ask for hush money.

It was the day after Jonathan left. Winnie knew the time was soon, she was at the point where she should have called for the doctor. In her mind, she worked out what she would say to Dr. de Malades after the fact. "It all happened so fast, doctor, there wasn't time to call you."

It's a mystery why most babies prefer to enter the world at night. Perhaps, they have no say in it. Maybe, it's impulse or instinct or something in our nature we can never understand. What is the secret of the night…is it the draw of the moon? The cover of darkness to hide what we truly are? For whatever reason, new souls prefer the middle of the night.

The house staff heard the madam's howls of pain. No matter how hard or often they pounded on madam's door, they could not gain access.

"Is everything all right? Should we send for Dr. de Malades?"

"No, don't you dare!" Ma Cherie shouted through the door. "All of you go back to your rooms. If I need you, I'll call you. Now, go away!"

Winnie did all she could not to scream, biting down hard on the edge of her pillow. The waves of pain swept over her, never giving her a chance to breath other than in a screech.

Ma Cherie questioned their judgment. "Maybe, we shouldn't take a chance? We should call Dr. de Malades."

"No…don't…you…dare!" Winnie shouted between gasps for air.

The clock rang three. Winnie was breathing heavily with nary a whimper. She felt exhausted, as limp as a wet rag. Ma Cherie changed the sheets soaked with sweat, wet as if left out in the rain.

"It's coming! You need to push!" Ma Cherie whispered.

"I can't!"

"You must!"

Winnie did what she could, though she exhausted most of her strength.

"It's coming…it's coming," Ma Cherie said. "I can see the head. Don't stop now, just a little bit more!"

In the next quick moment, Winnie's large belly flattened like a balloon deflating. A baby cried, shattering the silence of the late hour in the night. William Gibbs entered the world.

Ma Cherie held the child, inspecting him from head to toe. Winnie tried frantically to sit up and see what was happening, except she was too done in. Using a warm wet towel Ma Cherie washed the baby clean. She wrapped him firmly in a blanket and then placed William into Winnie's arms. He immediately stopped crying.

"That's a good sign," Ma Cherie said. "Nobody likes a fussy baby."

"Is he all right?" Winnie asked, sounding desperate.

"I gave him the once-over. It seems everything is as it should be, one of everything he needs to have one of, and two of everything he's gonna need two of."

Winnie let out a strong sigh of relief.

"Look, Ma Cherie! He's as white as his father! Oh, thank God!"

"Most babies come into this world light-skinned, darling, even black babies. For the most part they often need a few hours and then some need a day or two to see what they're really goin' to be. We'll know soon enough. Just be thankful he's healthy." Ma Cherie declared.

That was not what Winnie wanted to hear.

William began fussing, again. Winnie lowered the shoulder of her nightgown, placing the child to her breast. The boy began to suckle, as naturally as the sun rises in the east.

Winnie looked at her son at her breast. The smile left her face.

"Oh, Lord," Winnie cried softly. "He looks just like my father."

****

All day long, William did what newborns do. Mostly, he slept, when he wasn't nursing. And of course, there were moments of loud harsh crying. Thankfully, it wasn't often, still, there were times.

The house staff was in a constant state of alarm, knocking on the bedroom door, asking if anything was needed, if there was anything they could do. Each time, Ma Cherie sent them away.

"Should we call the doctor?" they asked more than once.

"No, no doctor," Ma Cherie ordered loudly, standing in the madam's bedroom doorway. "Don't talk to anyone."

They left all meals on the floor before the bedroom door. They were to knock and then leave. Their suspicions grew. It became the gossip of all the houses staffs in the neighborhood. Something was amiss, and they were itching to find out what.

At the end of the day, as William slept in his mother's arms, she examined him, slowly and carefully.

"He looks more and more like my father with each passing hour, and my father was a dark-skinned man, darker than anyone else in the family."

Without a word spoken, both Winnie and Ma Cherie knew where this was heading.

Winnie concluded there was nothing left to do other than carry out her plan.

All the preparation rested on the shoulders of Ma Cherie. First, she prepared one of the carriages, intending to make the journey alone, that is, just her and the baby. Using a small wooden crate, she lined it with blankets, in place of a crib. She filled the back of the carriage with as much supplies as she could.

Late in the night, while the household slept, she went to the farthest part of the back property. There, under a large widespread maple tree, using a shovel, she dug a small grave. When it was deep enough, she filled it back up, patting the soil back down, first with the shovel and then pounding her feet. For all purposes, it looked like a grave, the grave of a child.

Ma Cherie stood at the foot of the bed, as Winnie said her good-bye to her son.

"I'm asking one last time. Do you really want to go through with this?" Ma Cherie asked sternly.

Winnie just shook her head. Tears began to flow from her eyes, down her checks, onto he son.

"Forgive me, William. Momma loves you. She's doing this because she loves you. Don't worry; you will be back as soon as I can arrange it." She stopped speaking, sobbing uncontrollably.

Ma Cherie came along bedside, gently taking William from her arms. She stood, holding the child, staring at Winnie.

"You don't approve of me, do you?" Winnie asked through tears.

"Oh, I approve of you," Ma Cherie replied. "I think you're a good woman with a big heart. And I know you think you're doing what's best. But I don't approve with this whole scheme. A child belongs with its mother. You've got a husband who loves you and wholeheartedly devoted to you, yet, you lie to him. As well, you're turning your back on your heritage and your race. By denying your own blackness, you're dishonoring your own people."

Ma Cherie stopped for a moment, her face softened.

"If after all I've said, you still feel the same then I can't point a finger at you. We just see it from a different place. I may think you're wrong, only, like I said, I think you're doing this from your heart, and you think it's best. So, I won't mention it again. Just remember, in time all things done in the dark will come into the light. A lie is a spark, and a spark in time can burn down a forest."

With that, Ma Cherie and William left the room. Winnie buried her face deep into her pillow, weeping.

Outside, Ma Cherie placed William in his makeshift crib, covering him with another blanket to keep him from the night's chill. He was sleeping. Not to disturb him, she drove slowly. The journey would be longer this way, yet safer.

It took nearly an hour just to reach the edge of town. She looked back over her shoulder. The moon reflected in the water of the harbor. The city was asleep. She felt like a thief in the night making her getaway.

At the halfway point, William began to fuse.

"There...there, child," Ma Cherie said softly. "I know you're hungry. It won't be much longer."

She began to sing softly, which calmed him, lulling him back to sleep.

> Be not dismayed whate'er betide
> God will take care of you
> Beneath His wings of love abide
> God will take care of you
> God will take care of you
> Through everyday, o'er all the way
> He will take care of you
> God will take care of you
> No matter what may be the test
> God will take care of you
> Lean, weary one, upon His breast
> God will take care of you
> God will take care of you

Michael Edwin Q.

Through everyday; o'er all the way
He will take care of you
God will take care of you
He will take care of you
God will take care of you

Eleven

More Important Matters

The sound of wooden wheels creaking and burrowing into the dirt road startled Jolene. She rushed to the front door, looking out at the horizon. The sun's light framed the oncoming carriage, making it impossible to see who it was. As the horse and carriage entered the shadow of the trees, Jolene could tell the driver was Ma Cherie. She was alone. This meant only one thing. She was bringing the child.

Jolene started walking across the field, waving to Ma Cherie. When they were close, the two smiled at each other, incomplete smiles, smiles mixed with sorrow.

Ma Cherie continued driving to the house. Jolene walked alongside.

"So, how have you been?" Jolene asked.

"...tolerable, and you...?" Ma Cherie replied.

"All right...a bit lonesome."

"I imagine so," Ma Cherie said, surveying the house in the middle of a flat field with nothing else other than the sky and far-off trees.

Inwardly, both women felt awkwardly foolish. Skirting the issue with all this small talk, they fully understood the situation, yet, avoided it.

At the house, Ma Cherie climbed down from the carriage. It was time to face the music.

"Is it a boy or a girl?" Jolene asked.

"It was a boy. His name is William," Ma Cherie answered back as she walked along the carriage.

As soon as she lifted the sleeping child from his makeshift crib, he woke and began crying.

"He's hungry," Ma Cherie announced. "He hasn't eaten since late last night."

"Let's go around back, and get some goat's milk," Jolene said guiding them along the side of the house.

There was a pen around back. Jolene entered. The goat and kids ran to her. She purposely spent time each day with them, so they'd become used to her, preparing for this very moment.

Ma Cherie stood outside the pen, holding William, as Jolene milked one of the goats.

Both women felt a strong urge to say something. There were so many questions to ask. Yet, somehow they moved about in this silence, a silence that filled their ears, making their minds race.

Stepping out of the pen, carrying the bucket, Jolene walked to the house, followed closely by Ma Cherie. William's fussing was beginning to subside.

After feeding William, Ma Cherie went out to the carriage; she came back with the makeshift crib. Once she placed him in it and covered him, he fell asleep.

"I'm sorry, this is as close to a crib as I could find," Ma Cherie apologized.

"That's all right," Jolene answered. "There a small town walking distance from here. Winnie's been good about sending supplies and money. I'll just go buy one."

"That reminds me," Ma Cherie added. "I brought some supplies. There in the back of the carriage."

The two women sat down; finally, willing to talk, to say the words they both knew needed saying, as well as answering the questions that lingered over their heads like a great stone held by a fine thread.

"Tell me, how is Winnie?" Jolene asked.

"That's a difficult question to answer," Ma Cherie responded. "There was little trouble with the delivery. She's gaining her strength back swiftly. As for her heart, it's heavy, clearly on the road to being broken. I don't want to speak about her soul. That's between her and her creator. Still, let's just say I fear for it."

"What about Jonathan?"

Ma Cherie took in a deep breath, letting out a long sigh, before continuing. "The poor man is away on business. He's under the belief that his son isn't due for another week, he expects to come back to a peaceful happy home. Only, he's returning to a world of hurt and sorrow, a world where his son died the minute he came into it, and now buried in a cold grave under a tree in the backyard. At least, that's what she's gonna tell him. I feel sorry for the man.

"Oh, my dear Jolene, I'm full of fear. We are all living a lie. In the end, all will come to light. I fear that moment more than death. When the truth becomes known, and it will be, it will destroy everything and everyone in its path.

"When Jonathan learns the truth, will he be able to ever trust his wife, ever again? Could he remain with such a woman?

"Then there's you, poor Jolene. How much can you endure?"

"In my heart, Winnie is my dearest sister. I would do anything for her," Jolene snapped back.

"I understand," Ma Cherie said, "that's because you are like me, with no life of your own. What happens when you get a life of your own, and this all becomes an unfair sacrifice?"

Jolene had no rebuttal, seeing things clearly, having no leg to stand on.

Ma Cherie pointed to the sleeping child at their feet. "What about this poor child? What will become of him? Will he have a mother...a father...a future? When they placed the baby Moses into the river, things were as bleak as they are for this child."

Unable to speak, Jolene reached out for Ma Cherie's hand. They looked sadly into each other's eyes, and then turned their gaze to the sleeping baby.

A long chilling silence covered them like a blanket of newly fallen snow.

"I'm sorry you have to do this alone?" Ma Cherie finally said.

"Oh, it's not so bad. Like I said, there's a small town walking distance from here. There's a church there. The people are so friendly. I go to service every Sunday."

"Do you think that's wise?" Ma Cherie questioned. "How are you going to explain that suddenly you have a newborn?"

"I thought about that," Jolene responded. "I'll tell them my niece grew sick in childbirth. Now she's unable to care for the child, at least till she gets well. She had no family, except for me. There was nobody else, and I was willing to take the child in."

"That's fine, Jolene. Just remember, one lie always leads to other. You need a good memory, if you're going to lie. There's nothing to remember, when you tell the truth."

Again, more silence.

Abruptly, Ma Cherie rose from her chair. "I need to get goin'. I need to get back."

"Are you sure? You can stay the night, and leave in the morning."

"No, I need to get back before Jonathan returns, which might be today."

They stepped outside. Jolene helped Ma Cherie empty the back of the carriage of the supplies. When they finished, they sorrowfully hugged good-bye.

"I'll pray for you," Ma Cherie whispered into Jolene's ear.

"I'll pray for you, too," Jolene whispered back.

Slowly backing away, Ma Cherie climbed up into the carriage. There was time for one last exchange and a smile, and then Ma Cherie turned the carriage around, driving away.

Jolene stood in the doorway, watching as Ma Cherie disappeared over the horizon.

All thoughts vanished, as a newly-hungry William cried from within. She rushed in, taking him up in her arms. It was then the sadness of it all brought her to tears. She shook the notion from her mind. There were more important matters. It was time to milk one of the goats.

Twelve

Lies and Truth

Jonathan hired a carriage at the station. He was so excited to be home, he didn't wait for the driver to take his baggage down. He threw open the front door, flying into the entrance hall.

Some of the staff were there cleaning. They looked up; when they realized who it was; they deterred their eyes from him to the floor. Taking up their rags and mops, they left, without a murmur. Jonathan sensed something was wrong. The smile left his face. It was then Ma Cherie entered, walking toward him.

No words were needed. One look at her solemn face told him something wasn't right.

"What' happened?" he asked, his low voice trembling.

She moved forward, her arms outstretch, as if wanting to comfort him, still, she kept her distance, giving him his space, looking deep into his eyes.

"Jonathan, you need to remain strong…for your wife's sake."

He backed away from her, fear taking over. He looked up to the staircase.

"Winnie!" he called out, running up the stairs, two steps at a time, stumbling, and then getting up. At the top of the stairs, he rushed to their bedroom door, booting the door open, he entered, finding Winnie asleep in bed.

"Winnie!" he shouted, waking her. She sat up, staring blankly at him.

"Winnie, are you all right?"

"I'm fine, darling."

"What about the baby?"

She held her arms out to him. "Come to me, Jonathan."

He ran to her, falling on her, his head to her breast, her heartbeat filling his ears.

"It happened so suddenly," she whispered, stroking his hair. "There was no way of getting word to you."

"What was it?" he asked softly.

"Don't put yourself through more pain, Jonathan."

"I need to know."

It took her a moment. She talked slowly and clearly. "It was a boy."

"Where is he? Where is my William? Where is my son?"

"Don't do this, Jonathan."

He sat up, looking into her eyes.

"I need to know."

"He's already buried, my love. Under the large maple out back, it's peaceful there."

He dropped his head back down on her. She began again to stroke his hair, as he cried.

She whispered over him. "Go ahead, my love, cry. My tears have all dried up. Cry for both of us."

It pained her to see him in so much pain, the pain she inflicted on him.

She looked up to see Ma Cherie standing in the doorway, shooting a cold stare of disapproval.

****

"Yes, who is it?" Winnie addressed the knock at her bedroom door.

"It's Dr. de Malades. May I come in?"

She knew eventually he would visit. She prepared for his coming, in her mind; still, turmoil ran through her blood.

"Come in, doctor."

It was the middle of the day. The delivery left her weak. She was resting in bed dressed in her nightgown. Dr. de Malades walked to her bedside.

"How are you feeling?"

"Much better, doctor, thank you."

Placing his satchel at the foot of the bed, he gave her a quick once over, pressing on her throat glands, pulling her eyelids up, and looking down her gullet.

"I'd say you'll be just fine," he decided.

"I was thinking of getting dressed and getting out of this room, tomorrow."

"I can't see why not," he agreed. "As long as you take it slowly for the first few days, you'll be fine."

Just then, everything changed. It was as if all the air in the room disappeared. The smile left the doctor's face, replaced by a solemn stare. His voice went soft, yet firm, as a father might talk to a daughter, lovingly though stern.

"Winnie, what happened? Why didn't you call me?"

It took a moment to gather her thoughts.

"It all happened so fast. It came on me so suddenly, just ask Ma Cherie. Before we knew it, the child arrived, but he wasn't breathing."

"Jonathan tells me you buried the child in the backfield under a tree."

"I know it seems hurried. I just was too heartbroken and confused. I had Ma Cherie bury him."

Now it was his turn to take his time to gather his thoughts.

"You do know, Winnie, I'm obligated by law to investigate any deaths I come in contact with. I have to examine the body, confirm the cause of death, fill out a death certificate, and submit it to the powers that be."

Winnie's eyes went wide.

He continued, "There's only one way I can do that. I'm afraid I'll have to exhume the body. I'll have to dig up the grave."

"No!" Winnie shouted up at him. He looked at her with shock and disapproval. Realizing this called for a softer approach, she calmed down, changing her tone, whispering. "Doctor, please don't. I can't tell you what weight that will bring on this household."

"I'm sorry, Winnie, the law is the law."

She jumped out of bed, rushing across the room to a chifferobe. Taking a jewelry box, she returned, standing before him.

"I beg you, doctor, please, don't do this thing. What is done cannot be undone. The sorrow it will cause Jonathan will be immeasurable, not to say what it will do to our marriage. Please, reconsider."

She opened the jewelry box. It was filled with a queen's ransom, all the gifts given to her by Jonathan. She held the open box to him, offering it.

"Here, take what you want! Take it all; only don't do this cruel thing."

She stood before him, trembling, tears flowing from her eyes.

He reached out, closing the box, gently pushing it toward her.

"If it means that much to you, I won't."

"Thank you, doctor, thank you."

"You realize this means I'll have to falsify the death certificate, something I've never done in all my years as a doctor."

"Thank you," was all she could say.

He moves passed her. "Don't ever mention this to anyone, not even your husband."

"I promise," she whispered, not turning around.

"We'll never speak of this again," he said as he left the room, not looking back, closing the door.

Thirteen

Lies and Truth

Jonathan fell off the deep end into an ocean of sorrow. He was not himself. No longer the man he was. His entire demeanor changed, acting so unlike his true self, a man possessed by regret, an empty shell where a soul once dwelled, now burned away by the flames of self-blame.

He seldom went to his City Hall office, the times he did his mind was elsewhere, not on his work.

At home, he ignored everyone, including Winnie. Often, he remained locked in the parlor, sitting in the dark, never so much as lighting a single candle. He seldom ate; when he did it was barely a mouthful. What was most distressing was that he began to drink. He was never a drinker, whiskey in small amounts made his head spin. Now, he was drinking enough to make a larger man tipsy, only, it was never enough to make him forget. When he became drunk, he'd walk out the back door, across the field to the maple tree, falling to his knees, crying for hours over the grave of his son. The whiskey bottle always at his side, he'd cry and sip till he fell down unconscious, face down on the grave.

He withdrew into his own private world, a silent world of pain that he allowed no one to enter, not even Winnie.

To watch him in this state was torture for Winnie, for she blamed herself, and rightfully so. After days of watching Jonathan suffer, when it became too much to bear for either one of them, she made a vow, secretly within. She would sit with him, trying to talk him back; using all the love she could gather for him. If that didn't do it, if that failed, she would tell him the truth. Even if it meant losing him, even if it made him hate her, casting her out, she'd tell him the truth. She'd fall at his feet, beg forgiveness, if need be, even so she swore to tell him the truth.

****

Late in the night, Winnie stood at the door of the sitting room, holding a single lit candle.

"Open up, Jonathan. Don't shut me out, please," she pleaded. She pressed her head against the door. "I love you," she whispered through the door.

She could hear him moving around, and then walking to the door. He opened it.

"I love you, too," he claimed with tears in his eyes. His speech was slurred; his body swayed like a sailor on the deck of a ship in a sea storm.

She reached out to him. He took her hand, leading her into the room. The room was dark; the light of her candle illuminated their faces. From the window, the full moon hung in the sky, the moonlight haloed around Jonathan.

"I love you, Jonathan," she repeated. "Our love is strong. It can overcome this. Don't leave me, Jonathan. I need you."

He took the candle from her, placing it on a nearby table, and then taking her into his arms.

"I'm sorry, my love," he whispered into her hair. "I'm so sorry and ashamed. Please, forgive me. This will never happen again. I love you."

She reached up and kissed him. Tears rolled down her cheeks, not only because she had her husband back, it was because he said the words she should have said all along.

****

After feeding and a few soft lullabies, William fell asleep. He was good that way; he fused little, always easy to please. After more than a week, they were getting along splendidly.

Jolene finally got to sit when she heard a rapping. It wasn't coming from the front door; it came from the back window. She rose to investigate. There was the smiling face of Reverend Anderson. Jolene opened the window.

"Phillip, what a pleasant surprise, what are you doing here?"

He lifted his right arm, holding a large basket. "I was hoping we could have lunch together, find us a shady tree, maybe we could have a picnic?"

"Thanks, that sounds like fun, Phillip, but I'm afraid I can't, I have a guest."

"Well, she can come, too," he said, still smiling, trying not to look disappointed.

"It's not a she, it's a he," Jolene stated

The smile on Philip's face remained, yet clearly forced, almost painful, as difficult as trying to push a mule uphill.

"Well, he can come, too."

"I don't know," Jolene replied. "He's sleeping; I'm afraid to wake him."

The smile on his face disappeared like a rain cloud blocks out the sun on a summer's day, quickly and completely.

"I'll tell you what," Jolene said. "Stay there; we'll come to you."

She closed the window. He could hear her talking. "Wake up, William; we're going on a picnic."

As disappointed as he felt, he was able to reprimand himself. He was a Reverend and a Christian, and he would act like one. Whoever this William was, he'd treat him with respect.

Jolene turned the corner of the house, walking toward him. In one arm she carried a blanket, perfect for picnicking on. In her other arm was William.

She handed William to him, the child cooed softly, still in a daze and sleepy.

"Philip, this is William. William, this is Philip."

Philip broke into roaring laughter.

"When you said you had a visitor…when you said…I thought…"

"I know what you thought," she said, smiling knowingly.

They found a tall shade tree on the edge of the woods. Philip laid the blanket on the ground and the basket on the blanket, helping Jolene and the baby down.

"So…?" he said nervously.

Jolene took it from there. "So, you want to know what I'm doing with William? He's the son of my niece and…"

She stopped midsentence, knowing what she scripted to say, however, she was unable to continue. She liked and respected Philip. If anything would come from their friendship, she refused to hinder it with a lie. Softly, she began again."

"That's not the truth, Philip. I don't want to lie to you. I had a speech all planned out to tell you and anyone else who asked. But, I can't, especially to you. I'll tell you every bit I can. Please, don't ask me anymore. This is the child of a very close friend of mine. She's in trouble. She's asked me to take care of William for a time."

"She must be a close friend, for you to do this?" he asked.

"Yes, she is. She's like a sister to me. I'm sorry I was going to lie to you, Philip. I…I…"

"Say no more, it's all right," he said softly.

At that moment, two hearts opened, touching each other. Jolene respected Philip for being a gentle understanding man, and him admiring her for her honest and high moral character.

William was fully awake and cooing, sounding almost as if he were giggling.

Fourteen

New Direction

Lake Lery was a far ride from New Orleans, nevertheless it was worth it. It was a lovely part of the country. Few folks lived there, even less visited, making it for a calm day to spend on the shoreline. The drive, though long, was pleasant, on a winding road, clinging to the shore of the Mississippi.

Life at the Gibbs' home approached normal, a new normal, for sure; still, it was becoming pleasant, once again.

They decided to spending a long day together, away from the cares of the world, would do them good. Winnie and Jonathan packed a picnic basket, took one of the carriages, and headed for Lake Lery. It would be just the two of them the entire day.

Reaching for Jonathan's hand to help her down from the carriage, she looked to the lake and beyond.

"Why…it's beautiful."

Placing a blanket on the ground, they sat on the shoreline; the only sound was the water sloshing with the geese honking off in the distance.

Neither of them felt a need to say a word. It was such a pleasure to spend a quiet time together. Still, there was a question floating around in Winnie's head. When she felt the time was right, she asked it.

"Jonathan, you never told me what the Governor spoke to you about."

"I've been meaning to tell you. It just didn't feel like the right thing to do at the moment. I guess now's as good a time as any."

"Start at the beginning. I want to hear everything," Winnie said, making herself comfortable.

"Well, there's not much to say. The train ride was without incident. When I got to Baton Rouge, I checked into a small hotel not far from the Capital, big building the Capital, it looked more like a castle than a government building.

"I had an early appointment with Governor Johnson. I was on time, but I still had to wait more than an hour. He's so busy, you know? He was a nice man, made me feel right at home.

"We talked for hours. Later we went to a restaurant with some of his cabinet; we talked until late in the night. The next day, I returned to his office, to work out some of the details."

"Details...details of what? Why did he call you there?" Winnie asked, growing excited and impatient.

"Well, I guess the long and short of it is he wants me to run for mayor of New Orleans, and he's willing to back me."

The news stunned Winnie. Her eyes and her smile went wide. "Oh, darling, that's wonderful. I'm so proud of you."

"Now, hold on," Jonathan laughed. "He's just asking me to run. I have to think about it."

"What's to think about?" she questioned his judgment.

"Winnie, you need to understand what kind of a life you'd be in for. The election is more than a year away. That's a year of hard work, hours upon hours, I mean, days of hard work, not to mention all the sacrifices. And it comes with no guarantee. Who's to say I'd win?"

"You'll win; I just know it. Jonathan, I have so much faith in you. I'm so proud of you. I'm willing to sacrifice for you, if you're willing."

"It'll be hard on our marriage," he warned.

"It couldn't be more of a trial than we've already gone through," she said.

They both knew what she was talking about; the moment went cold, neither one of them wanting to go any deeper into that issue, again.

"Very well," he concluded. "I'll wire Governor Johnson the first thing in the morning; I'll tell him it's a go."

"Oh, darling...!" Winnie shouted, flying across the blanket into his arms.

****

After William's morning feeding, Jolene wrapped him well, and then started walking to Sans Nom. She knew the child slept after feeding; he was a deep sleeper. Perhaps, she could take the child with her to the church service without incident.

Outside the barn...the church, that is, Jolene took in a deep breath to calm her nerves, before entering. It worked for only a second. On entering, all heads turned. Their eyes went wide with curiosity, on seeing her with a newborn in her arms.

Jolene made her way to the front of the congregation to stand alongside Celene. She smiled at Jolene. There was no hint in Celene's eyes of questioning. Obviously, Philip told his sister in advance what to expect.

It was a fine service with good singing and preaching. Something Jolene missed in her life, and was grateful for.

As before, the congregation gathered outside. That was when all the attention was on her and William. Questions flew at her faster than she could answer them.

"His name is William. A close friend of mine is having serious problems. I promised I'd watch over William till she is in a better place and can reclaim him."

Jolene stuck with this story. It felt good to repeat it because in a sense it was the truth. However, she became evasive on many other questions.

"Why…he's beautiful. May I hold him?"

Nothing is more annoying than to be sleeping comfortably and have someone wake you and then move you, only to get comfortable once more, and then repeat the process, again and again. William began to bawl at the top of his small lungs.

"I better take him," Jolene said, taking William back into her arms. "I best be going home. He's probably hungry."

"There's no need to go," one of the women declared. "I'm sure there must be someone here who could wet-nurse him."

Jolene disagreed with many of Winnie's requests. Refusing William a wet nurse was one of them. Nevertheless, she saw no harm in respecting this one.

"That's very kind, only I have a ways to go to get home. It'd be better if I just leave now."

As she was walking away, Philip ran to her. "Jolene, where are you going?"

"Oh, William's getting hungry and I'm getting tired. I best be getting home."

"Then, I'll walk you home."

She smiled up at him. "Thank you, Philip, only this is your church. You need to be here…for them."

"Well then, may I call on you tomorrow?" he asked like a young schoolboy, so shyly and humbly. She couldn't say no to him, even if she wanted to, which she didn't.

He leaned forward, smiling at her. There was a moment she suspected he would kiss her. He didn't. For his sake, she was glad he didn't, yet it would have been nice, she thought.

"See you tomorrow!" he said, walking slowly backwards a few steps towards the others.

"Tomorrow," she called back as they both turned, he to his flock and her to her home.

Fifteen

Postponed Plans

"Your mama's coming for you. We're both going home," Jolene whispered to the child in her arms, looking out the front door, seeing a carriage approaching. Even from a great distance, Jolene recognized the woman seated in the back was Winnie.

Jolene stood in the doorway holding William. When the carriage stopped out front, Winnie didn't wait for help down. She ran to Jolene, taking William up in her arms like a person coming up from the water gasps for air.

To not let the carriage driver see, they ran inside the house, closing the door behind them.

Winnie held no idea she would be so emotional. She'd missed her son; however it wasn't until that moment she realized how much. She paced the floor, crying with the child in her arms. The movement and the noise upset the child. William took to a fit of wailing.

Winnie tried to consol him, "It's all right, William, momma's here." This only frightened the boy more; he cried all the louder. "What's the matter with him?" Winnie asked, looking worried.

"You're upsetting him. Here let me," Jolene said, taking William from her. In familiar arms, he went silent and calm.

Winnie felt like someone tore her heart from out of her chest. Her own child didn't know her, he felt safer in another's arms. She burst into tears. "He doesn't even know me!"

"It will all be all right," Jolene said softly. "Once he get's used to you, it'll be like you never were apart."

Jolene's words of encouragement moved Winnie, which made what she came to say all the more difficult.

Jolene placed William down in his crib. "It won't take me long to pack. I don't have much. Only, what should we do about the goats. I guess we could set them free."

Winnie reached out, stopping Jolene. "Jolene, that's not why I came, I'm here to see my son, nothing more."

"I don't understand." Jolene said, as much a question as a statement.

"I was planning to have you return. I honestly did, Jolene. Except, something's happened. The Governor asked Jonathan to run for mayor. Isn't that wonderful! So, you can see the timing is all wrong. We need a little more time. We'll have you come back, as soon as it's possible."

"One of your house staff goes off and comes back with a baby. What harm could that cause?" Jolene disputed.

"So soon after losing my own child, it might cause talk."

"But William *is* your child."

"That's just what I mean," Winnie replied. "It's just the wrong time. We need to get through this election, first. We'll have you and William back home, as soon as it's over."

Jolene stood staring at Winnie. "Do you not know what you're saying? Do you not hear yourself? I don't understand you. One moment you're crying how your own baby doesn't know you, the next second you're cutting yourself off, again."

"I'm doing what I have to do, no matter how hard it is," Winnie argued "I'm doing this for all of us."

"Don't put me in this," Jolene said. "I have nothing to gain by this fiasco. You keep saying it's for the good of all. You know, I'm beginning to doubt that. Each time I see you, you're getting more and more like the old Winnie."

"Please, Jolene, don't say those things," Winnie begged humbly. "I don't want anything to come between us. You're my dearest, closest friend, and I love you."

"I love you, too," Jolene replied, "but I don't understand you."

"Please, Jolene, let's not talk about this anymore. It'll be over soon, we'll have you back before you know it. Please, I came here to see my son. Let's not ruin it."

It was true, it was time to drop the subject, neither one would ever change the other one's mind.

Winnie took William up, again. Immediately, he started to cry.

"You need to support his head with your hand. Like this," Jolene said, guiding Winnies hand in place. William stopped crying.

"You see," Jolene said. "It's all going to be fine."

Sixteen

Contrary to Popular Belief

Alain Naudé was good at his work, in fact he was the best, although, his job description was vague, to say the least. Perhaps, it would be better to explain what he did, as opposed to giving it a name. Alain Naudé was an expert in elections. He could change the course of votes, redirect them, forge them, as well as make them appear or disappear. In short, the candidate who hired Alain to run his campaign made an extremely smart move. Governor Johnson wired Jonathan of the arrival of Naudé with specific instructions to follow every command uttered from the mouth of Naudé.

Alain's bloodline was mostly French with a droplet of Cajun. So, spending a year in New Orleans would be like coming home for him. He was middle-aged, an uneventful looking fellow, single all his life, for good reason. What mattered most to him was work. Socializing was a waste of time, as were many of the ordinary and commonplace parts of life that most people relish in, he appalled.

He was short, pale skinned, balding with a few nearly invisible strands of white hair. Clearly intelligent, when speaking all eyes turned to him as he spoke with a commanding tone that was hard to resist.

Jonathan offered Naudé office space at City Hall. Alain declined, stating the least connection he had with Jonathan and his family, and the public, especially news reporters, would be ideal. This was worrisome. Jonathan was not one to hide his light under a bushel. Anything that needs doing in the dark was usually something one needn't or shouldn't do.

He also declined Jonathan's offer to stay at their home. Again, stating the least contact and connection between them the better. So, Jonathan arranged for a small townhouse for him, walking distance from City Hall, as well as the Gibbs' home.

Alain's first night in town, Jonathan invited him to dinner. Alain declined, however, asked for an audience with Jonathan and Winnie in private at their home the following day. He also specified to have the house staff not see him. Again, this was not only strange but troubling.

Midmorning, Jonathan and Winnie met Naudé at their front door.

"Would you care for something to eat?" Winnie offered, pointing towards the dining room.

"Thank you, Mrs. Gibbs, I've already eaten. Besides, there's much we need to go over, first. Is there a room we can talk in private?"

"Yes, right this way," Jonathan said, leading them to the sitting room.

"Actually," said Naudé, "I like to speak with Mrs. Gibbs first, alone."

"Yes, of course," Jonathan said, backing out of the room.

"Please, close the door as you leave, Judge Gibbs," he asked gently though firmly.

"If we're to work together, please, call me Jonathan."

"I think it best we remain more formal, Judge Gibbs. If it will make you feel more comfortable you may call me Alain."

Jonathan closed the doors of the sitting room, as he exited; feeling more unsure of what he'd gotten himself into.

It was clear from the start; Naudé would be friendly, yet not familiar. His manner was clear, he was in charge.

Alone in the sitting room, behind closed doors, he remained standing, waiting for Winnie to take a seat.

"Would you like something to drink, Mr. Naudé.?" Winnie asked.

"No thank you, Mrs. Gibbs. Please, be seated."

"You may call me Winnie, if you like," she said as she sat on the sofa, making the same mistake as her husband.

He smiled, as he took a seat on the sofa across from her, clearly not taking the gesture seriously.

"We'll use that name wisely," he stated. "Winnie is a common name, much too informal. When we are dealing with the common folk, we may use it to our advantage. I imagine your real name is Winifred. We'll use that name whenever needed. But with the quality people of New Orleans, you must remain dignified. We will always address you as Mrs. Judge Gibbs. Always remember to include the word *Judge*, as it instills an air of confidence and power."

Winnie didn't even try to hide the distaste she held for this statement. One look at her face, Naudé knew what she was thinking. He took in a deep breath and then let out a long sigh before expressing his intent.

"Mrs. Gibbs, let me make one thing clear from the start, so we know what I'm doing here. I help win an election, that's what I do. I'm not here to be your friend, your wise uncle, or your loving father. I know what works and what doesn't. If I seem harsh at times, don't take it personal. We're all here to get your husband elected, right? Good! Now, that we understand each other, shall we begin, again?"

Winnie had no answer, she nodded.

"Contrary to popular belief," Naudé continued, "elections have nothing to do with politics, law and order, the common good, or even the will of the people. These are just a façade made of fools gold and cut glass. In truth, what elections are is a popularity contest. That is my goal, to make your husband more popular than his opponents, and both of you the most popular couple in New Orleans.

"However, before I can do that I need to know everything about both of you, singularly and as a couple. I need to know your strengths and your weaknesses, your good points and your bad points."

This took Winnie off guard. "What do you mean the good and bad of us? What does that have to do with anything?"

Naudé let out a muffled laugh. "You sound like someone with something to hide, Mrs. Gibbs."

This threw Winnie into a state of worry and deep discomfort.

"I need to know the good about you so I can promote you. I need to know the bad about you so I can keep it hidden."

"Why even bring it up?" Winnie asked.

"My dear innocent child, if we don't nip any regrets from your past in the bud, your opponent will use it against you. They will search for anything they can hold against you, anything that will make you unpopular. To tell you the truth, we will be doing the same. We'll scour their past till we find dirt, and then we'll wave it like a flag for all to see. It's a dog eat dog business. We need to head off any bad publicity before it starts. So, Mrs. Gibbs, I need to ask you questions. Please, answer honestly."

This turned Winnie to stone with freight.

"Let's start at the beginning," Naudé continued. "Tell me about your family. Where were you born?"

Winnie remained silent, unable to answer.

"It seems we've stumbled on a problem," he announced.

"Mr. Naudé, I'll tell you as much as I can. To be honest, my past is shady, to say the least. My family was poor folk. Once I was on my own, I did what I needed to do to survive. My life before Jonathan is a dark past, indeed. If my past were to be known, they would surely use it against us," she concluded, using all her courage and strength to say that much.

"I see," Naudé commented. "No need to tell me anymore. I understand fully, Mrs. Gibbs, I'm not judging you, however, the public will. As I said, your husband's opponents will do everything in their power to dig up whatever dirt is out there on either one of you. So, I suggest we invent a past for you as soon as possible, and get it out there for all to hear and believe. When this campaign starts, all will know your glorious background and never need question it."

"Such as. . .?" Winnie asked.

"I'm not sure. I'll need some time to not only make up a good story; I'll have to devise a way of getting the story out there. Perhaps, a few newspaper articles and local gossip will do the trick? That shouldn't cost much. Now, if you could please leave, and ask your husband to step in, that would be most helpful."

Winnie left with her tail between her legs, which were shaking. If her true past ever became known, all would be lost.

"Are you all right?" Jonathan asked, as she walked passed like a solemn ghost, expressionless, save for her blank stare.

"He wants to see you. . .now," was all she could say as she started up the staircase.

****

Jonathan's life story was a dream come true for Alain. Every detail was perfect. His family tree stood cluttered with law-abiding, respectable, industrious, wealthy, entrepreneurs. His father was a well-known respected Judge in New Orleans. He'd followed in his father's footsteps, doing him one better, becoming the City Judge. His mother was the strong silent force behind her husband, active in the community and church, liked by all. Still, there were questions needed to be asked.

"Judge Gibbs, I have some delicate questions I need to ask. I'm just doing my job. So, if none of this applies to you, please, don't take offense. However, if it does, I need you to answer honestly."

Jonathan nodded.

"As a judge, have you ever taken any bribes?" Naudé asked matter-of-factly.

It was clear Jonathan took offense to this.

"Judge Gibbs, I told you to brace yourself. Now, if you have, your opponents will find out and use it against you."

"No, I have never taken a bribe," Jonathan said bluntly.

"Do you have any illegitimate children?"

This went through Jonathan's heart like a sword of fire. Just the word *children* brought to mind the loss of his son. Nevertheless, he brushed his feeling aside and answered.

"No, I have no children." The words dripped coldly from his lips.

"Affairs…have you had any affairs?"

"Affairs…?" Jonathan questioned the question.

"Have you been with any women you shouldn't have been with, especially married women?"

"No, I've never had an affair."

Naudé looked Jonathan squarely in the eye. "Judge Gibbs, there's no need to lie to me. I'm here to help. I've never known anyone, least of all a politician, that didn't have something in their past they didn't want brought into the light."

"I'm sorry, sir," Jonathan said. "What can I say? My family raised me right."

This statement rubbed Naudé the wrong way, finding it offensive. Still, being a true professional he shrugged it off with no visible signs of annoyance.

Not believing his good fortune, Naudé burst into laughter. "It's a shame, sir; you're in politics instead of the clergy. You'd be up for sainthood."

****

When he finished his initial investigation, Naudé asked them both into the sitting room for his findings.

"I'll take that drink, now, Mrs. Gibbs," Alain said, once the three of them settled in the sitting room, Winnie and Jonathan sitting across from him.

Winnie poured three brandies, passing them out, and then sitting next to her husband. They looked to Alain with anticipation.

"Let me lay this out plainly," Naudé started. "Judge Gibbs, your profile is perfect. My job will be to get it out to the public. This will be easy; moreover the cost will be minimal. Don't worry; all expenses Governor Johnson will take up, on your behalf. All he expects in return is that you work with him and treat him fairly once you're elected. And you will be elected, sir, I guarantee you.

"Mrs. Gibbs, you've indicated to me you have a checkered past. Have no fear, I'm not going to press you for the information, and I will make sure no one else does. I will do this by creating a past for you, something honorable with a touch of mystique. Once I've done this, I will put your story out there for all the public to see, just as I will your husband's.

"Once completed, I will publicize you as a couple as well, in good standing, admirable, interesting, popular, and most of all attractive, which you are.

"When I get all this in place, it will be time to announce your candidacy. The best way to do this is to throw a gala here at your home. We'll throw the most fabulous party in the history of New Orleans, inviting only the upper crust. Again, the Governor takes care of all expenses.

"Now, if you'll excuse me, I'll be on my way," Naudé said, abruptly standing and then heading for the door. "Thank you, again, for your hospitality. Once I get matters in order, I'll report to you by means of the post."

With that, in the next eye blink, he was gone.

Winnie reached out, placing her hand on her husband's. "Oh, Jonathan isn't it exciting."

"I suppose," he replied, reluctantly. "I don't like the idea of the Governor picking up the tab. I have a hard time believing all he wants in return is for me to be fair in my dealings with him."

****

Dear Mr. and Mrs. Judge Gibbs,

It was a pleasure meeting you the other day, as I am sure it will be so working with you both. All that we spoke about, I have put into motion. I have contacted all the prominent reporters and news outlets in the city. The guest list for the gala is coming along well. I've also been speaking with caterers.

If we move quickly with this, you will be first to put your name in the hat for the mayor's race, being the first gives us a head start, which is good.

I put much thought into the background of Mrs. Gibbs. Please, memorize it, as once this is made public, you surely will be questioned on it. Mrs. Gibbs biography is as follows:

Mrs. Gibbs was born Winifred Cummings, the only child of Derik and Monica Cummings. Her family can be traced to her great, great grandparents coming over on the Mayflower. Her grandparents moved to New Orleans, investing in import and export merchandise, including the slave trade. Thus, the family fortune and destiny was sealed.

After the passing of her grandfather, her father took charge of the family business. Winifred grew up in a happy home, loved by all. Her education was in the good hands of private tutors, until the age of sixteen, when she was sent to Le Meilleur finishing school for young girls in Baton Rouge. (Have no fear; I've secured your name in the list of alumni.)

On a Christmas visit, Winifred met Jonathan Gibbs at a church function. The two were immediately smitten with each other.

Everything after that was done properly and in the open. Judge Gibbs, a lawyer at the time, asked Winifred's parents' permission to court their daughter. A year later, he asked for her hand in marriage.

Sadly, before the marriage, both Winifred's parents became victim to the cholera epidemic that scourged our fair city, at the time.

Winifred Cummings, soon to be Mrs. Judge Jonathan Gibbs, was the sole heir of the Cummings' business and family fortune. Because of his dedication to law and order, his life's calling; Judge Gibbs refused ownership of the Cummings' fortune, and sold all assets with most of the proceeds given to charity.

Over the years, Mrs. Gibbs has proved to be an inspiration to women everywhere, standing firmly behind her husband at every turn. If ever there was a woman destined to be First Lady of the fair city of New Orleans, it would be Mrs. Judge Gibbs.

Sir and Madam, this is what I plan to submit to the newspapers. If either of you can think of anything that needs adding or omitting, contact me, immediately. Again, both of you must memorize this completely. As for the incidentals such as names and places, have no concern, I know how to cover my tracks.

Humbly,

Alain Naudé

Both Winnie and Jonathan were speechless for a moment. All of a sudden, Winnie exploded with laughter. "My family made their fortune in the slave trade!"

Seventeen

Special Places

Everything about Jolene's life, within and without changed. The way she thought about the world and about the way the world thought about her. Her entire universe was altering, and for the better.

Before moving in with Winnie and Jonathan, life for her was a nightmare. Living with them was a dream come true. She lived comfortably, secure without any fear. Who could ask for more? Only, you can ask for more. It is the human experience that must always move forward or dissolve. Life is change; how it differs from the rocks.

Now, there was more to her life, more than just being content. Now there was hope, excitement, things to look forward to, dreams to dream, and reasons for living.

The cottage with all the touches she put in, it now felt like home, no longer a guest. It was her home.

Caring for the goats, in time, she could easily be considered the envy of any shepherdess, and she enjoyed it, as well. She even gave them names. Whenever she came to feed or milk them, they ran to her.

Her friends numbered many. In time, she got to know everyone at church. There were dinner parties with neighbors and a few at her home in response. If she needed some time to herself, mothers with children offered to sit with William, in return for her childcare services. The ebb and flow, the give and take of love within friendship is a blessing, and one of the needs of life such as food and air.

Other than the new joys in her life, there were three people that found a special place in Jolene's heart.

Celene and Jolene became close, as close as sisters, just as it was with Winnie, only there was steadiness about Celene that made her seem older and wiser like an older sister would. Someone with a steady temperament that you could rely on and ask advice of; as well, it worked both ways; there was nothing Jolene wouldn't do for Celene. Being with Celene was like being with family.

Jolene always felt excited being with Philip, when it was just the two of them, especially. He was always a gentleman.

It went unspoken that each had an eye for the other. They spent time together after church services, many visits to her cottage as well as countless picnics, alone, save for

William. Her growing feelings for Philip were a surprise for Jolene. Romance was something she believed would never be in the cards for her. Over years of abuse, she learned to guard herself, treading lightly around men. Excluding Jonathan, she never met a man of higher morals, someone she could trust, feel safe with, and enjoy their company. Philip was just such a man, and more. He could make her laugh; make her think, and best of all, smile. They became closer with each meeting. It would be fair to say, although Philip was always a gentleman, she began entertaining thoughts of him perhaps being not so much so.

When he spoke to her, often she would focus her gaze on his lips, wanting to kiss them. Wanting to dive into his arms and lose herself in them. These were the thoughts that would appear in her mind's eye. What could she do? Women must play the waiting game, and Philip was so cautious. She daydreamed when he would throw all caution to the wind.

As stated, there were three people, new people who found a home in Jolene's heart. The third was William.

He was a beautiful child, and all folks easily find a soft spot in their heart for such a child. Jolene was no exception, only that's not where it ended, only where it started. The flow ran both ways. In time William captured Jolene's heart, totally.

As he grew so did his personality. When she held him in her arms, he'd smile up at her, a smile that belonged to the two of them; it was a smile he reserved for her alone. When she nuzzled him, he showered her with angelic giggles. The joyous look he gave her when she walked into a room, the same one he threw across the room to her when seeing her face mingled with no matter how many others. A simple lullaby captivated him like an aria from a Rossini opera. Leaving him lost in sleep, unable to distinguish between good and evil, in a dream of calm loving.

Recognizing this bond between them, Jolene would make herself scarce whenever Winnie came to visit. William, a good-natured child, would have a pleasant visit with his mother. Winnie enjoyed these visits, never knowing what her son was capable of, to connect as he did with Jolene.

Sad to say, Winnie's visits became less frequent, as Jonathan's election campaign took up more and more of his and her time. Till finally, only a weekly delivery of supplies, money, and a short letter, brought by one of the drivers, could be expected.

Jolene's heart went out to Winnie. She realized that in her foolish beliefs Winnie was doing what she thought was best, denying her husband his own son, not to mention she was missing one of the great joys a woman could ever know. For this reason, Jolene wrote to Winnie every week, describing in detail little William's day-to-day adventures.

Alone in her bedroom, Winnie would read these letters through tears. She kept them hidden in a hatbox under their bed.

Eighteen

Where There's Smoke

It was not only his job, it was the way he saw the world, everything in details, steering the ship away from the rocks.

Alain Naudé made sure every aspect was perfect, starting with invitations to all the right people, the wealthy and the influential, the upper-crust of the city in business and in politics. As well, he saw to all the things that make for a successful party, extra staffing, and the best food and drink the Governor's money could buy. He hired the finest musicians playing nothing that would be too loud or obtrusive. He even considered the lighting and atmosphere. Nothing was too difficult or two small, and everything in its place.

He not only made sure that everyone who was anyone received an invitation, people of influence and affluence not only in New Orleans but also in surrounding counties. One never knows where or when favor would be needed.

Alain Naudé was a shrewd man. He went so far as to invite the potential competition, such as Louis Philippe de Roffignac, the then Mayor of the city who was surely considering running for another term, and many other potential candidates. The backing Governor Johnson, both publicly and financially, was sure to shake up the competition, if not persuade some to reconsider their candidacy and back out, all together.

Naudé also took the liberty of picking out what clothing Winnie and Jonathan were to wear to the Gala. Jonathan, thinking it strange was not comfortable with being treated like a child. Winnie on the other hand felt deeply disturbed about being told what to wear. Her mistrust and dislike of Alain Naudé was becoming noticeable and difficult to bear.

At Alain's orders, Winnie and Jonathan stood near the front door, greeting the guests as they entered. It was all done formally with the widest and mostly false smiles, especially by those who would later run against Jonathan. They were the ones with the largest smiles, pasted on their faces the entire night. Mayor de Roffignac and his wife were perfect examples of this technique. As if planned and not by chance, they were nearly the last guests to arrive.

"Rumor about town is saying you're thinking of running for mayor, and that you have the backing of the Governor behind you?" Mayor de Roffignac asked through smiling gritted teeth.

Not wanting to go into long-drawn-out particulars, Jonathan's answer was as simple as possible. "Yes, that's true, and yes, the Governor is behind me."

This cut the mayor's smile to half its size. Being a professional politician, some of it remained. His wife was a different story, her smile disappeared, her face went cold, her expression cruel, as her eyes shot out poison daggers. If looks could kill, Winnie would have died instantly when the two women faced each other.

"That's a lovely necklace you are wearing tonight Mrs. de Roffignac," Winnie pointed out, hopping to melt some of the ice between them.

"Oh, this old thing, it used to belong to my mother. If it didn't have sentimental value I'd never wear it. It's so cheap and tacky."

This was a direct cut at Winnie. Both women knew what she wore was far more expensive and luxurious than what Winnie wore. Saying it was cheap and tacky was another way of saying what she wore was more so. When it came to cattiness, Winnie could bite and scratch with the best of them. However, for her husband's sake she would avoid the woman like the plague. There would be no great loss there.

Not thinking it interesting, Winnie had never looked at the invitation list Alain composed, before he sent them out in the post. If she had, she surely would have protested, desperately avoiding what was about to happen.

The past was about to return with a vengeance.

While greeting the Mayor and his wife, Winnie looked up to see who was next in line.

With one look, Lot's wife turned to a pillar of salt. Winnie feared the same fate.

The next guest in line was the infamous Madame Charbonneau, looking as beautiful as ever. The two women locked eyes. Winnie's jaw dropped, as Madame Charbonneau's lips pealed apart framing her ever growing grin of perfect pearl white teeth.

Though not as overcome as his wife, Jonathan was nearly as surprised, only for a different reason. Madame Charbonneau's reputation preceded her, a reputation of being someone to never trust, an evil person, to say the least. Still, she was a woman of wealth and power, which, he assumed, was why Naudé invited her. Not being a good time to question, Jonathan played along. He reached out, taking Madame's hand.

"Thank you for coming," he said with a smile, including a slight bow.

"Thank you for inviting me," Madame Charbonneau replied with an equally large smile and a slight curtsy.

There was sweetness in Madame Charbonneau's voice, thick and syrupy as honey. It charmed men, leaving them weak, at her command. However, a woman can hear what it truly is…a siren's song…a tactic of the seductress.

When the two women stood face-to-face, Winnie was unable to respond. A cold wind ran through her, causing a paralyzing chill. Jonathan gently prodded her, nothing. Finally, Madame Charbonneau reached out taking Winnie's hand.

"It's an honor to meet you, Mrs. Gibbs. I've heard so much about you…all good, I might add," she said, adding levity, which was lost on Winnie. "We need to talk later. Something tells me we're going to be good friends."

Madame Charbonneau walked into the heart of the party, disappearing. Winnie knew it was impossible, yet, it seemed as if Madame Charbonneau's grin still hung in midair before her.

"Darling are you all right?" Jonathan whispered. "You look like you've seen a ghost."

****

Nothing brings out enthusiasm in people as a full belly and a head full of wine. After all the guests arrived, and everyone had drunk at least one drink or more, Alain had the musicians stop playing. He stood smiling, waiting for the room to quiet. When he was sure he had their attention, he made his announcements.

"Ladies and Gentlemen, we are so pleased to have you here tonight. We do hope you enjoy yourselves. However, before we start, it gives me great pleasure to introduce to you your host and hostess, Mr. & Mrs. Judge Gibbs."

The crowd applauded, as they stood before everyone. Taking their lead from Naudé, they waited for the crowd to settle.

Jonathan held Winnie's hand as he spoke. "My wife, Winifred, and I welcome you to our home. We want every one of you to have a grand time, so I'll make this short. I am throwing my hat in the ring. I will be running in the next mayoral election."

There was a burst of cheers and applause that lasted a good minute or more. This was not a sign of any real enthusiasm; it was just considered good manners. All eyes turned to Mayor de Roffignac and his wife to see their reaction. Being a true politician, de Roffignac politely applauded with his wife, showing no response, letting everyone know he wasn't fazed in the least. Of course, this was all for show. Inwardly, his mind was racing, and of course Naudé knew this, it was his job to know. Mayor de Roffignac bowed his head slightly to Jonathan who returned the nod. Although, looking on the mayor's wife's face told a completely different story – again, as they say: *if looks could kill.*

Just then, Alain stepped between Winnie and Jonathan, holding up a letter with the state seal on it.

"I have here," Alain announced loudly for all to hear, waving the sheet of paper in the air, "an endorsement for Judge Gibbs' campaign from none other than the Governor!"

It was perfect timing. If anyone had any doubts about whom they were going to back, those doubts dissolved. You can tell the winner at the starting gate; everyone loves a winner.

"Enough politics for one night," Jonathan shouted over the dim. "Welcome to our home. Eat, drink, and be merry!"

There was another howl of approval from the crowd. When the roar simmered down, they took Jonathan at his word, eating, drinking, and mingling. On the other hand, there were those who understood politics never really stop. Those who would be affected by a Gibbs' candidacy, talked among themselves, each in turn would corner Jonathan before the night was over, pressuring him for more information.

Not so strange, it was the same with the women. Although, many women congratulated Winnie, there were many who had a million questions to ask, prompted by their husbands.

Alain did not remain idle. He went about weaseling his way into small groups of men talking and drinking. He made sure each of them got to examine the accolades written by the governor about Judge Gibbs, as he preached the wisdom of backing this unexpected dark horse.

The women gathered around Winnie, bombarding her with questions, few of them political.

"What a lovely home you have, Mrs. Gibbs, did you do it all yourself?"

"That dress, that dress, I must know where you got that dress."

"I know real pearls when I see them; they are real, aren't they?"

Winnie's head was swirling from all the attention, twirling about, smiling back at each smiling face. That is, until the face before hers was that of Madame Charbonneau. The smile on Winnie's face left her faster than if someone slapped it off. A dark cloud covered them both. A frost ran through Winnie's veins like an out of the ordinary icy breeze left over from the winter, attacking her.

"What's the matter, dear?" Madame Charbonneau asked in a low kindly voice. "Someone walk over your grave?"

"What are you doing here?" Winnie asked through gritted teeth.

"Don't you know, dear, you invited me? This is all very exciting. I'm thinking of backing your husband, myself."

"That's not what I meant, and you know it," Winnie grunted.

"Now, is that anyway to treat an old friend?" Madame giggled.

"What do you want?"

"You were always a smart girl, Winnie. Oh, I'm sorry; it's Winifred, now, isn't it? Either way, you know exactly what I want. You've done extremely well for yourself, my dear. None of it would have happened without me. I believe this makes me entitled to some restitution, wouldn't you say?"

"How much…?" Winnie whispered.

"How much…? My dear Winifred, don't be so crude."

"I want you out of my house, this instant."

Madame moved in uncomfortably close to Winnie, close enough to whisper in her ear, "Tomorrow, at my place at one o'clock. I assume, you still remember the address."

Madame Charbonneau turned, mingled into the crowd and a moment later was lost. Winnie saw the back of Madame's head as she exited the front door.

Before Winnie could collect her thoughts, more of the women were surrounding her with more questions.

"Are you and your husband planning to have any children?"

Winnie just smiled.

****

"I'm going to have to speak with Naudé, tomorrow," Jonathan announced as he pulled the covers back and got in bed.

"Why what's wrong, it was a perfect evening?" Winnie asked, reaching across the bed to him.

"It's that woman, Madame Charbonneau. I can't believe he invited her. I realize she's wealthy, except she's not someone we want our campaign associated with."

"Why, what's wrong with her?" Winnie asked.

In the second Winnie asked this, her mind pondered back to when she confessed her past to Jonathan. She couldn't remember if she told him about the connection between her and Madame Charbonneau and her time at the school. If she had, perhaps, Jonathan did not remember her ever mentioning the association. Either way, Winnie let out a long sigh of relief when she realized he knew nothing of their connection.

"I'll tell you what's wrong with her," Jonathan explained. "She's no one we need our name linked with. I've heard some things about her that would make your skin crawl."

"Perhaps, it's nothing but rumor," Winnie cut in.

"They can't be all rumor," he continued. "Even if only half of what I've heard is true, she's a despicable person. Anyway, you know the old saying: *Where there's smoke there's fire.* Now, let's get some sleep. It's been a long day; I'm suspecting they all will be long from now on."

Inwardly, Winnie was glad to put the whole Madame Charbonneau thing behind them, even though she planned meeting the women the next day in secret. Nevertheless, that was a bridge she'd worry about when crossing it. She rested her head on his chest, listening to him breathe.

"Just think," she whispered. "I'm sleeping with the future mayor of New Orleans."

Jonathan laughed softly, as he pulled her in closer.

Nineteen

Something Important

Talk throughout the congregation was that Pastor Philip and Jolene were smitten with each other. Though they never heard it directly, if they had, neither one of them could deny it...because it was true. The infatuated way they acted when around the other was not only obvious it was comical, like two youths in awe of each other.

From Sunday to Sunday, not a week went by the two didn't spend time together at least three or more times. There was, of course, Sunday service, the church activities, dinners together, Philip and Celene at Jolene's home, or Jolene at their home. And there were the countless picnics the two enjoyed together.

It was on one such picnic; Philip fearfully tossed his fate to the wind, hoping it would come back tenfold.

They let little William crawl about the picnic blanket. The good-natured child laughing each time he bunked into something.

"Have you heard from William's mother, lately?" Philip asked.

"Yes, she sent me a letter. I'm afraid she's still not able to care for William."

"That's too bad," Philip remarked.

He sensed Jolene had given him the short answer. If she didn't want to talk about it, he wasn't going to press the point, so he changed direction.

"He's getting so big," Philip commented.

Jolene's smile grew. "I was just thinking the same thing." She reached across the blanket for William. "I'm gonna get cha...I'm gonna get cha," Jolene sang out, as William burst into laugher similar to the chimes of Christmas bells, as he scooted away from her.

They played with William till he slowed down; inevitably, falling fast asleep, which was the moment Philip waited for.

He reached across, taking Jolene's hand. She stared down at their hands, speechless.

"I have something important to say," Philip said softly. "You've come to mean so much to me. My feelings for you have grown. I must tell you my intentions are honorable. My purpose is to pursue you, my intent is marriage."

Within Jolene it was the Fourth of July, complete with a brass band and fireworks, outwardly, stunned and speechless.

"Jolene...Jolene," Philip called her back to earth. "What do you say to this?" he said, sounding more like a prayer than a question.

He looked at her stone-faced, suddenly a smile appeared on her face, and relief and joy rushed through his veins.

"So, you'll consider my proposal?"

"Of course, I will, Philip. I think you're the kindest, sweetest, smartest man I've ever known."

"I was hoping you'd throw good-looking in there, too," he said shyly.

"Yes, and that, too," she laughed.

They sat silently, Philip looking at their entwined hands, smiling, seemingly pleased with the outcome.

"Well...?" Jolene asked, breaking the silence.

"Well, what?" Philip asked, sounding confused.

"Well," Jolene explained. "Usually when two people come to a major understanding they do something to signify the moment. Some people shake hands to seal the deal, others sign a contract. Although, I think neither of these would be appropriate."

"Then what would you suggest?" Philip asked.

Jolene grinned. "Oh, I do hope you're putting me on. I know you're quick on your feet. I've seen you."

He smiled knowingly, leaned in close, taking her in his arms, they kissed.

Jolene could hear her heart pounding.

It was a short kiss, as they both burst into laughter when they heard a giggling William trying to be a part of it all.

Twenty

Drop in the Bucket

"Mrs. Judge Gibbs to see Madame Charbonneau," Winnie said through the bars of the front gate.

Without a word, the guards opened the gate. They'd been expecting her. One of the guards escorted her into the house and down the long hall.

Nothing had changed. The sight, even the smell, of her old school rushed her senses, bringing her mind back to that time in her life.

She'd tried so hard to forget the past, and now it all came flooding back. She was not prepared for the memories that stirred in her, none of them good recollections, sending chills through her body.

When they came to that familiar door, the office door, they stopped, the guard knocked gently. "...Mrs. Gibbs to see you, Madame."

"Show her in," Madame called out, her voice oozed through the door in that familiar honey-like tone, slow and overly sweet.

Winnie stepped inside; the guard closed the door behind her. She stood before Madame Charbonneau, seated behind her large mahogany desk. Madame waited for the sound of the guard's footsteps to fade.

"Winnie! So good to see you, please, sit down. Would you like some tea or something to drink?"

Winnie stepped forward, refusing to sit down. She shot daggers from her eyes at Madame.

"Stop it! Just, stop it!" Winnie shouted. "We're not friends, we never were friends, and this is not a friendly visit. We know why I'm here, so, let's drop the charade and get to the point. What is it you want?" Winnie placed her hands on the desk, leaning forward, only inches from Madame's face. "Oh, by the way, if you think you can threaten me with telling my husband about my past, well, you're too late, I've already told him everything."

Madame leaned forward, smiling at Winnie. "Good for you," she exclaimed. "It's good to see a marriage based on honesty and trust. It's a rare thing, nowadays. I do wish you'd sit down, you're giving me a stiff neck," Madame said laughingly.

Winnie backed away slowly, her eyes fixed on Madame, as if she were backing away from a snake. She took a seat.

"So, what is this going to cost me?" Winnie demanded to know.

"As you may imagine, I love money as much if not more than the next person. However, money's only a drop in the bucket, only a small part of what I want," Madame replied. "If your husband wins and becomes mayor he's going to be a man of power. Power is even more important than money. Society has many rules and regulations, many laws. If you husband wins the mayoral election, your husband will be in charge of those laws. I just happen to be a woman who enjoys going against the law. I find it more to my liking and far more profitable. To have your husband on my side would be heaven-sent."

"And what if we don't play along?" Winnie asked.

"Then you don't get to play at all," Madame laughed. "You won't even be in the game. So, your husband knows of your past, good for you. Do you have the slightest idea what will happen to your husband's campaign if the city knew *your* past. How you were a Fancy, a mistress, a prostitute, and most of all, your heritage, that would be the end of his career as a judge, let alone a mayoral candidate. You'd probably need to leave the city, hell, you'd have to leave the state," Madame laughed for a moment, and then continued. "And remember I have people that would gladly testify against you in court."

"You're despicable," Winnie snarled.

"Yes I know," Madame laughed, again. "And remember, I have photographs of you in not so endearing poses."

"Is there any amount I can offer you, so you'll back off?" Winnie asked.

"Never," Madame replied. "Like I said, money is only a drop in the bucket. I plan to have a long and fruitful relationship with your husband."

Realizing it was useless to argue any further, Winnie rose from her chair, starting for the door.

"I'll be in touch by the post," Madame called out.

Winnie gave no response, continuing down the hall.

"What? Not even a good-bye," Madame shouted. "Some people can be so rude," she hollered, exploding into laughter, so loudly that Winnie could hear her even after she stepped out of the front door.

****

"Madame, Mrs. Mélangé is here," the guard announced after rapping gently on the office door.

"Send her in," Madame called out.

90

Mrs. Yvette Marie Mélangé stood before Madame, just as Winnie had only a few minutes before, wearing the same forlorn expression.

Mrs. Mélangé was in trouble. The *Sword of Damocles* weighted heavy and low overhead, and the person holding that sword was Madame Charbonneau. Much of what happens to us in our lives is directly affected by the choices we make, and Yvette had made all the wrong ones. It was easy to see why.

She was young, far too young to be on her own. She was so naïve, not innocent, mind you. That was something she lost a long time ago. Although, she was sophisticated, knowing about the finer things in life, what to wear, art, manners, what wine goes with fish and so on. Still, she felt lost outside her own little world. Some might call her simple minded to a fault, yet that never held her back in life.

Being young and beautiful since childhood and from a wealthy family can be an asset. However, when the world accepts you for *what* you are and not *who* you are, the inner character seldom receives feeding, stunting its growth.

She had made all the wrong choices, and now she was to pay for those choices, and nothing, not even her beauty or wealth could help her.

"You know what will happen to you, if I release those papers," Madame said coldly.

Mrs. Mélangé just nodded.

"I like you, Yvette," Madame said, her tone softening. "I'd hate to see a life so young ruined. So, I've decided to return them to you, to do whatever you want, burn them, for all I care."

Her head bowed low, staring at her shoes, a look of hope sprung in the eyes of Mrs. Mélangé. Now, she looked up, a smile appeared on her face.

Then Madame dropped the other shoe.

"Except first I want something from you, Yvette."

The look of hope disappeared from Yvette's eyes just as fast as it appeared. Her smile faded like morning vapor on the grass. She knew this was not going to be easy. Especially, when it came to dealing with Madame Charbonneau, a woman who would sell her mother, let alone some young member of the aristocracy.

"How much money do you want?" Yvette asked.

"Money…? Why you insult me, dear girl."

The young woman tilted her head in wonder.

"I want you to do a little job for me, first," Madame continued. "How long has it been since your husband passed?"

It was the talk of the town when Yvette married a man old enough to be her father...no, her grandfather. Those who knew her intimately knew she married for money, and couldn't wait for him to die. She felt it a blessing the old man fell over dead six months into their marriage. If he hadn't, she feared she would have to murder him. She was glad fate spared her that.

"Less than a year," Yvette replied. She'd stopped wearing morning black garb months ago.

"Less than a year...?" Madame reacted. "It seems longer. Well, anyway, you're single, young, rich, beautiful... What man in his right mind wouldn't have you?"

"What are you asking?" Yvette asked frightfully.

"I want you to seduce a man for me."

"I can't do that," Yvette said, sounding more like a plea.

"Of course, you can."

"Who...?"

"Are you familiar with Judge Jonathan Gibbs?"

"I've heard of him, that's all."

"Well, Judge Gibbs is running for mayor in the next election. I've got the goods on his wife; if I had something on the judge, too, I'd have them both in the palm of my hand. I've looked into his political background, he's squeaky-clean, never a scandal. There's never been a scandal in his entire family. How boring. So, we'll have to make one up. I want you to seduce him, and once we have it well documented, I'll approach the good judge with it."

"I don't know how to seduce anyone."

"Oh, you'll find a way, I'm sure."

"What if I can't seduce him?"

"That's your problem, not mine. Just remember, if you don't succeed, I hand over those papers to the authorities, and you know what that will mean."

"Can't I just pay you? I'll pay whatever you ask."

Madame laughed. "I've got all the money I need. Power is what I want. Now, get out of my sight; don't contact me till you've succeeded."

"If I do this, will you give me back those papers?"

"Get out," was Madame's final order.

****

Judge Gibbs,

You do not know me; I'm sorry to intrude on you, but you are my only hope. This is a matter of life and death, too delicate to communicate in a letter. I'd visit your office, only, I'm afraid of the scandal that may ensure.

I beg you, come to my home, so I may tell you of my plight. I am available between the hours of three and six. Tell no one.

Yours Expecting,
Mrs. Ronald Mélangé
503 Napoleon Avenue

Twenty-One

That's Not What We Planned

"Is that it?" Ma Cherie shouted, pointing at the lone cottage.

"That'd be it," Winnie confirmed.

Ma Cherie complained so much and so often about missing Jolene and not seeing baby William that Winnie agreed for her to come along, if she promised to drive the carriage. Ma Cherie was far better company than her usual driver.

As they approached, they saw Jolene standing in the doorway, waving to them. The two women frantically waved back.

Jolene was holding William, no longer in her arms, she held him on her hip. He had turned toddler. She took hold of his arm, shaking it up and down to look as if he was waving, also.

Winnie jumped out of the carriage, rushing to the cottage. Her first reaction was to take William from Jolene. The child let out a scream of terror.

"It's all right, William, it's mommy…its mommy," Winnie repeated, shaking the baby up and down in her arms. Jolene hurried to her side to intervene. With a few soft-spoken words, William calmed.

Ma Cherie ran to Jolene, the two women flying into each others arms, rocking back and forth, laughing.

William was peaceful, now, cooing and laughing from Winnie's gestures.

"Why don't you spend time with William, while Ma Cherie and I catch up with each other?" Jolene suggested to Winnie, motioning to inside the cottage. Winnie gleefully took William inside.

"Do you like goats?" Jolene asked Ma Cherie.

"Goats…?" Ma Cherie questioned.

"Come with me around back; I'll show you," Jolene said, laughing.

Winnie and Ma Cherie stood in the back of the house, staring at the corral of goats and kids.

"You weren't kidding when you said goats," Ma Cherie laughed.

"Winnie didn't want her son with a wet nurse. The only alternative is goat's milk. He actually likes it. Although, I'm starting to work solid food in to his eating habits, ground up real good, that is."

They both stared quietly at the goats for a few moments

Jolene finally spoke up. "So, how have you been?"

Ma Cherie thought deeply before answering. "As you know, I was against all this from the beginning, all these lies, William here with you, Mr. Jonathan believing his son is passed on. It's all so wrong, only, now there's something else. Ever since Mr. Jonathan announced his candidacy, there's another evil floating about. I can't tell you what it is, because I don't know. I ain't seen or heard it, so I can't put my finger on it. But it's there and it's just as real as me looking at you, right now. This family needs prayer and plenty of if."

"I've never stopped praying," Jolene replied.

Just then, Winnie stepped out of the cottage with William on her hip. "Ma Cherie, could you take William for a moment. I need to speak with Jolene."

"How have you been, little man?" Ma Cherie said, taking William from Winnie and entering the house.

Alone, the two women stood silently staring at the goats, until Winnie spoke her mind.

"My dear sweet sister, Jolene, how can I ever repay you?"

"It's been the pleasure of my life," Jolene responded.

"I'm glad you said that," Winnie answered back, smiling. "Because, I have another favor to ask of you, forgive me, I have no one else to turn to. As you know from my letters, Jonathan is going to run for mayor.

"Now, I know you must be dying to return home, and you will someday. I'm asking you to stay her with William just a little longer. With this election, everything is topsy-turvy. If you could please stick it out a bit longer.

"I'll keep sending supplies, and writing you, only, I'm afraid I may not be visiting as often, anymore. You do understand?"

"Winnie, there's no need to put yourself through this. I do understand. I will remain here, taking care of William, for as long as you ask me. Only there's something I need to tell you."

The tone in Jolene's voice was serious, downsizing the smile on Winnie's face.

"I will stay here with William as long as you ask," Jolene repeated before continuing. "Except, when the time comes for me to return, I'm sorry, I will not be returning."

"What are you saying?" Winnie asked. The smile erased from her face.

"I love William as my own, but he's not, he's yours. Whenever you call to have him back I will bring him. Except, I can never go back, it's no longer my home. I've made a life for me, here; this is my home, now; I will never leave it."

"But…but…" Winnie stammered in confusion. "That's not what we planned."

"That's not what *you* planned," Jolene snapped back.

"How will I ever explain taking a black child into our home?" Winnie pleaded.

"The truth might work," Jolene pointed out; only, this solution flew over Winnie's head, never entering her ears. "You'll think of something," Jolene remarked, trying to encourage her.

"It's a man, isn't it?" Winnie said mockingly.

"That's part of it," Jolene answered.

"Well, you can't stay here. This is my house, not yours. You'll have to get out." The next moment, tears welled up in Winnie's eyes. "What am I saying? Oh, Jolene, forgive me. I should never have said that."

She fell into Jolene's arms.

"I didn't mean it. I wasn't thinking. Forgive me. You can stay here as long as you want. I'll give it to you, if you like. If you've found someone, I'm glad for you."

"It's all right, Winnie. I understand, you're under too much pressure. There's nothing to forgive."

"What's his name?" Winnie asked.

"Philip Anderson, he's the pastor at the local church."

"That doesn't surprise me, knowing you."

They both broke into laughter.

"You do what you have to do," Winnie said. "I'll figure something out."

Winnie leaned forward, kissing Jolene's check.

"My dear sister," Winnie said.

"My dear sister," Jolene echoed.

Winnie turned heading back to the house. "Ma Cherie!" she called out. Ma Cherie came to the backdoor, William smiling on her hip. Winnie opened her arms, as she approached. "Let me spend some time alone with my son."

Ma Cherie handed William over to Winnie. They entered the cool of the cottage. Ma Cherie, once more, stood next to Jolene.

"So, how many goats do you have?" Ma Cherie asked. "And who's this Philip fellow?"

Jolene turned to Ma Cherie in surprise. "You were listening!"

Ma Cherie laughed loudly. "Of course, I did. You'd be surprised the things a person gets to hear."

Jolene gave her a gentle look of disapproval.

"All right," Ma Cherie said, "you don't have to tell me about the goats. Now, who is this Philip?"

Twenty-Two

Don't Trust Anyone

Yvette Marie Mélangé was a magnificent beauty; no one who knew her would deny that. However, these same people would be the first to tell you she was the most spoiled self-centered person you would ever meet.

As an only child of a wealthy family, she learned to get whatever she wanted by manipulating those around her with her good looks and sweet voice. One could count on one hand the few times she ever heard the word, "No."

During her final year of finishing school, through a friend of a friend, Yvette met Ronald Mélangé. He was immediately smitten with her. Yvette remained unmoved, as she normally was by those other than herself. What did move her, though, was learning the amazing wealth that came with the man. They began courting.

Yvette's parents were against it all, him being many years her senior that is until they learned of the man's lineage and wealth.

A year later, Ronald proposed; the wedding day was set. They honeymooned at his family's vacation home on the Gulf.

They lived in Ronald's home in New Orleans, one of the largest grand mansions in the city. For all wants and purposes, it was a happy marriage. Yvette was his personal plaything, to love, cherish, and flaunt. For Yvette, Ronald was her personal bank, open all hours, day and night, allowing her to live the life she believed she was destined for and rightfully deserved.

Ronald was a man of many weaknesses, none of which were women, so he always remained faithful to his bride. Yvette remained true as well, only, for different reasons. She knew of no man wealthy enough to risk losing her luxurious lifestyle.

However, Ronald did have his faults. Those being gambling, a pastime that took him from his home for days with little sleep, heavy drinking, and his Achilles heel, opium and morphine. He'd spend days in dark basements, his mouth wrapped around the long black pipe, riding the dragon.

In the end, it all destroyed Ronald. Though, still a healthy man in most people's eyes, he died without warning. His heart simply gave out.

For weeks, Yvette wore the face of a mournful widow, although she felt more elated, now being one of the riches women in the state. Nothing could stop her, now. That is except Madame Charbonneau, the woman who held Yvette's future in her hands.

The reason for this hold on Yvette is too dark and nothing that need mentioning or discussion in moral society. It is best just to accept that it is so and move on.

The threats of Madame would continue, unless Yvette did her bidding. That was to use all her feminine charms to seduce Judge Gibbs.

****

Jonathan backed off slightly with surprise when the front door opened. He was expecting a butler or a maid to answer, instead it was Mrs. Mélangé.

"Thank you for coming, Judge Gibbs. Please, step inside," Yvette said, holding the door open and stepping aside.

Jonathan entered cautiously. From the start, he felt uneasy. He sensed something wasn't right. For one thing, there was no one else around, no servants, no sounds from the kitchen or any other room in the house.

"Don't worry: there's no one here, it's just the two of us," she said softly as she closed and locked the front door. The stated was uncalled for, mystifying Jonathan.

The other, and more disturbing, thing that made Jonathan uncomfortable was what she wore. Yvette stood dressed in a flimsy nightgown, covered in a sheer robe tied in a large bow in front. It was so revealing, Jonathan felt ill at ease just looking at her. He followed her into a large sitting room.

"Would you like something to drink, Jonathan? You don't mind if I call you Jonathan?"

He decided to put his foot down, firm, yet, still polite. "Mrs. Mélangé with all due respect, I'm here in reply to your written request, which if you remember, was concerning life and death. That was a weighty statement to make, which is the reason I'm here in the first place. Now, if we could just get to the point."

"I'm a widow," she proclaimed with a long sigh. "My husband died only a few months ago. Ronald, that's my husband, Ronald took care of all financial problems. He never even mentioned them to me. Now, here I am, on my own, with bills, contracts, mortgages, paperwork to the ceiling; I don't know what do to. I've heard you are a knowledgeable and fair man. If you could just go over these things for me, help me put my life back in order, it would mean so much to me."

"This is what you call 'life or death'?" Jonathan groaned. "Mrs. Mélangé..."

"Call me Yvette," she cooed.

He ignored her, pressing on. "Mrs. Mélangé, I don't do that sort of work anymore. This is a job for a lawyer. True, I was once a lawyer…" he stopped for a moment, "You do know what it is I do, don't you?"

"Yes, you're the City Judge."

"Correct, that means…" he stopped, again, realizing it was useless. "I'll tell you what I'll do. There are some fine lawyers in the city; I know a few of them. I'll pass your problem on and have them contact you. Now, if you'll forgive me, I must get back to my office. He heaved a sigh, turning to the door.

"Jonathan, no, don't leave!"

The sound of her calling him by his Christian name made him uncomfortable. Still, he stopped and turned, looking back at her.

"Mrs. Mélangé…?" he questioned in a formal tone to make it clear that under no circumstances were they on friendly terms.

"I lied," she moaned with her head bowed down, and then looking up, her soft doe eyes welling up. "I just had to meet you. I was at your announcement party. The moment I saw you, I knew I had to have you. Forgive me, I can't help myself."

Jonathan looked dumbfounded; he took in a deep breath, his lips tightened, as he started to turn once more to the door.

"Please, Jonathan, don't go!" she cried.

Fear came over him; facing her, he slowly backed away.

Suddenly, she reached up, undoing the large bow across her breasts. The nightgown opened; she slipped it from off her shoulders, dropping it to the floor, revealing her nakedness.

"I'm married," Jonathan proclaimed, backing farther away.

"No one will ever know," she said, reaching out to him.

"I will!" he declared.

Like Joseph running from Potiphar's wife, Jonathan rushed out of the room and out of the house. And like Joseph, in his hurry, he left an article of clothing, his hat. Proof he had been there.

****

The door opened slowly. Molly walked in at a snails pace, which was her way, being as shy as a small woodland creature. She was tiny, barely over one-hundred-fifty centimeters tall, weighing under seven stone. Her bones protruded through her flesh. Her eyes were sad and scared like her soul. Her hands were the hands of a slave, gnarled, scarred from hard work. Her maid outfit was as old and worn as she. She stood at attention; holding a man's hat, a charcoal gray, black headband, a John Bull, the height of gentleman's fashion.

"So, Molly, what news do you have for me, today?" Madame Charbonneau asked, looking up from her desk at the girl. Molly stepped forward slowly. "Well, don't just stand there, girl, what news have you?"

"I done like ya told me to," Molly said timidly. "I've been keepin' an eye on my mistress, Madam Mélangé. For the past week, she's been sending me and the others out of the house, sayin' don't come back till after six, which we done. Well, today, when we came back, I went to check on Madam Mélangé. I found her in her bedroom, lying in her bed, dead as a doornail. She done cut her wrists. I was going to call the police or somebody, and then I found this here letter next to her. I figured I best get it to ya, first."

"That's exceptionally smart of you, Molly," Madame Charbonneau said, standing up, reaching across the desk for the letter. "What does it say?"

"Oh, I don't know any readin'," Molly replied.

Madame opened the letter, reading silently.

My life is over. Everything is in ruin. Madame Charbonneau has my destiny in her hands, there is nothing she will not do to crush me, and there is nothing I can do to stop her. So, I go to where she and no one else can touch me, to my grave.

Madame folded the message, placing it into the top drawer of her desk.

"Does anyone else know of this," Madame asked.

"No, ma'am, I didn't tell anybody. I got the only key to her room. I done locked it, so nobody can get in."

"The hat," Madame asked, pointing the hat Molly held.

"I found it in the sittin' room. I swear it twasn't there when we left the house, but it was there when we got back."

"Give it to me," Madame ordered, reaching for it.

At first glance, it seemed just an ordinary hat. Indeed fashionable, a hat a young wealthy gentleman might own.

Closer inspection revealed more. Inside the hat, written on the leather sweatband were the owner's initials. This was not an uncommon practice, as many gentlemen wore the style of the day, making it easier to identify, especially at restaurants and gatherings where they left their hats at the door.

Reading the initials, Madame instantly knew whose hat it was.

"J.J.G," she whispered to herself, "Judge Jonathan Gibbs, of course. It seems the little tart did get him to come to her house. From the outcome, I'd say she failed. Being the stupid girl she is, she took the easy way out."

"I'm sorry, ma'am?" Molly questioned, not understanding.

"Nothing, none of your business," Madame snapped.

She opened the main drawer of her desk, took out a sheet of paper, a pen, and an inkwell. She also took a hundred dollar gold piece, handing it to Molly.

"A gold piece..." Molly said, mesmerized.

"You've earned it," Madame replied. "There's only one more thing that I want you to do."

"What's that?" Molly asked excitedly, willing to do anything short of murder, or perhaps not.

Madame lifted her finger, relaying she needed one more minute. Madame with pen in hand wrote on the sheet of paper. She folded it, handing it to Molly.

"I want you to go back to your mistress's body, place this note in the exact place you found the other note. Then I want you to scream bloody murder that you just found the body. Then I want you to call for the police. Do you understand?"

Molly nodded.

"Good, then repeat it to me."

"Ya want me to take this note and place it where I found the other note, and then call the police."

"Good. And when the police come they're going to ask you many questions. All you say is you found your mistress dead. Make no mention of the other note, the man's hat, and don't ever tell anyone you and I ever met. Do you understand?"

Molly nodded, again.

"Repeat it back to me."

"My mistress is dead, and I don't know nothin'."

"Very good, Molly, I may have work for you in the future."

"Thank you, Madame."

"Now, quick, before anyone else tries to enter the bedroom."

Molly was gone in a flash.

****

"Come in," Jonathan called out. His office door swung open revealing one of Jonathan's oldest friends at City Hall. It was George Savior, captain of the New Orleans police department.

George Savior was a middle-aged man, an unremarkable looking man, easy to dismiss and forget. As cold and cruel as that may sound, it was an asset to someone in investigating police work. Pretty boys find it difficult to trail a suspect; they stand out like a sore thumb. You need to blend in with your surroundings. George Savior was the last person you'd suspect was following you.

Jonathan was close friends with Savior when Jonathan was a mere lawyer. Now the City Judge and candidate for the next mayoral election, their paths rarely crossed, which was something they both regretted, still, one must follow one's calling.

"Wasn't expecting you, George, long time, no see, what brings you here?"

"I'm afraid it's business, Jonathan."

Jonathan's eyebrow went up. "Sit, George. What's this all about?"

Savior took a seat. His tone became official sounding. "Do you know the widow Mélangé, Ronald Mélangé's widow, Yvette Mélangé?"

"Yes…and no," Jonathan replied.

"What's that suppose to mean?"

Jonathan chuckled slightly. "Well, I never did know her until yesterday. It's all so strange. I've known you long enough to tell you. She sent me a letter asking me to her house, said it was 'life or death'. When I got there, she's wearing some flimsy nightgown, and her staff is gone. She tells me she needs legal help, so, I tell her I'll recommend a lawyer. Then she tells me the real reason she wanted me there. It was to have a love affair with her. To tell you the truth, George, it scared me to death. It was all too crazy, so, I got myself out of there."

Jonathan stopped his tale, looking to George in bewilderment.

"I don't understand, George, why are you asking me about Yvette Mélangé?"

Offering no explanation, George handed him a folded letter. Jonathan opened it, reading it silently.

My life is over. Everything is in ruin. Judge Jonathan Gibbs has been my lover for nearly a year. He has rejected me. So, I go to where he and no one else can touch me, to my grave.

Yvette Mélangé

"Where did you get this? It must be some sort of joke. I don't understand," Jonathan said.

"Of course, you don't understand," Savior replied. "It's a letter written to ruin your life. At first glance, one may surmise you were her lover, and then left her heartbroken. You left her so distraught that she committed suicide."

"Yvette Mélangé is dead?" Jonathan asked in shock.

"I'm afraid she is, and it's your fault, that is if you believe her suicide note."

"Do you believe it, George?"

"After applying some rudimentary detective practices, I was able to decipher what is actually happening here. Someone is trying to ruin your good name, which would destroy your chances in the coming election."

George placed the suicide note on Jonathan's desk, pushing it toward him to get a better look.

"The main problem is the paper is from someplace other than Madame's supply. The ink is also not of Madam Mélangé stash, as well, the letter is written by someone who is left-handed, and Mrs. Mélangé was not, she was right-handed. And lastly, no one refers to her lover as *Judge Jonathan Gibbs*. Obviously, whoever did write this note wanted to make it perfectly clear that you were the one who drove her to her death."

Jonathan still looked befuddled.

"Do you still have the letter from Madame Mélangé, inviting you to her home?"

"I'm not sure, let me look." Jonathan tossed a few papers about. "Ah, yes, here it is." He handed it to Savior.

Savior looked at it carefully, comparing it to the other letter.

"Just as I thought… This clinches it. The handwriting is from two different hands. Someone planted this suicide note."

"Who would do that?" Jonathan questioned.

"Don't you understand, Jonathan? You're running for the most powerful office in the city. Some folks are going to try to get some dirt on you so you lose the election, and others to hold power over you if you do. Whoever did this has a far-reaching arm."

"Yet, Yvette Mélangé is dead…why?" Jonathan asked.

"I guess we'll learn why, when we find who wrote that note."

Jonathan pushed the note across his desk, back to Savior.

"So, now what do you do?" Jonathan asked.

"Me…? First person I need to speak with is the maid who found the body. Although, I doubt I get anything from her. If anything, she's probably in on it and most likely the person who planted the note."

"What about me, what should I do?"

Savior laughed. "You...? You watch your back, and don't trust anyone, and I mean anyone and everyone."

Twenty-Three

There's Fire

Whenever Madame Charbonneau dined at Antoine's, the restaurant staff went all agog, up on their toes, eager to serve and please. Money has that affect on some people.

"Your usual table is ready, Madame," the maître d'hôtel announced, waving his hand toward the small table at the far end of the restaurant, next to the window. She enjoyed watching the parade of people as she ate. He held the chair out for her, making her as comfortable as possible. "Enjoy you meal, Madame."

"Tito, wait a moment. Who is that man?" Madam Charbonneau asked, pointing at a man on the other side of the pane, smiling at her.

"I wouldn't know, Madame. If he's disturbing you, I'll have him removed."

"Yes, please," was all she need say.

They sent one of the waiters to go out on the street and ask the man to move on. Madame could not hear what was being said, although she could see their lips move. After the waiter warned the man, the man must have said something to the waiter that stopped him in his tracks. The waiter's face turned pale. The stranger walked off.

A moment later, to Madame's surprise, the man who stood at the window was walking across the restaurant from the front door towards her.

"Madame Charbonneau…? I'm Captain Savior of the New Orleans Police. May I have a word with you, please?"

Madame was never one to become flustered. She remained her coolheaded, controlled, and gracious self.

"Captain Savior, please sit down. I've been expecting you."

"Really…?" Savior said, sounding amused, as he sat across from Madame. "You were expecting me, how so?"

"Do you play chess, Captain?"

"I can hold my own, why?"

"To succeed in chess, one has to think many moves ahead of their opponent. That's why I knew you'd pop up, eventually."

Savior snickered, "That deserves an explanation."

"Let me lay it out for you," she said, and then snapping her fingers at a passing waiter. "You…two absinthes, here…"

"I'm waiting," Savior insisted, keeping it friendly.

"You're investigating the Yvette Mélangé death, aren't you? One look at the suicide note, you knew it was a forgery. So, being a good investigator you interrogated the maid who found the body and the note. It didn't take you long to scare the poor creature into confessing the truth. That's were my name came up. Only, there's nothing you can do about that."

"Oh, you think not? It is the truth, you know?"

"All you've got is the word of a frightened little Colored maid against mine; that won't hold up in court or anywhere else, for that matter. As for it being the truth, does it matter? People will believe what they want to believe. You can tell them the truth all-day long, it won't make a difference. Shout it from the rooftops that Judge Gibbs never cheated on his wife. But where there's smoke there's fire, they will say. Just the rumor of being a liar will spread like wildfire, hurting his campaign to be mayor."

Just then, the waiter came with their drinks.

"You know Antoine's is one of the few restaurants where you can get true absinthe from Holland. I hear the government is considering banning the import of it. They say it corrupts the mind, thus corrupting the country's morals. I say the hell with morals. Life's too short," she proclaimed, taking a long sip of the green potion.

"Please, continue," Savior requested.

"What more can I say? With such a rumor floating about, Gibbs might as well throw in the towel."

"Of course, you have the proof to prove him innocent," Savior declared with more than a hint of sarcasm.

"You said that, not me," she replied coldly.

"And this proof is there for a price, I presume?"

"The term price suggests money. That sounds so cheap to me. Let's say it's tit-for-tat."

Captain George Savior finished his drink. "Got quite a kick," he commented, placing his hat back on his head, tipping it in respect. "Been an interesting time, I must say. Nice meeting you, Madame. I can now say I've met a true chess master. Don't take so long to convey your terms to Judge Gibbs, make it as soon as possible, before his campaign is damaged beyond repair."

"Don't say a thing to him. I'll be in touch with Mrs. Gibbs. Women are so much easier to deal with."

****

Walking down the center aisle of Cathedral-Basilica of Saint Louis flooded Winnie's mind with memories, both good and bad. She recognized Madame Charbonneau sitting in the front pew. Winnie sat down in the pew directly behind her.

"What's the matter, don't want to be seen with me?" Madame laughed.

"Let's just do this," Winnie demanded coldly.

"Do you have the money?" Madame asked.

Winnie didn't answer; she handed over a tightly packed envelope, which Madame stuffed in her purse.

"I thought you said you had no interest in money?" Winnie questioned in anger.

"That's true, I did say that. Then I thought, if he doesn't win the election, all this was for nothing. So, I figured money is better than a poke in the eye with a sharp stick."

"You'll do what you said you will; you'll clear my husband's name?"

"Of course, I will. Not out of the kindness of my heart, mind you. It's just that I plan for a long profitable relationship with you and your husband."

"Go to hell," Winnie spat out.

"Now…now, my dear, we're in a church, remember?"

Madame rose, starting down the aisle. Before passing Winnie, she tossed a man's hat next to her.

****

Madame Charbonneau was true to her word. She surely must have had friends in high places. The following day, every newspaper in New Orleans, and a few of the major papers around the state, ran an article proclaiming the innocence of Judge Jonathan Gibbs. How it was all a misunderstanding, how he was true-blue to his wife and office.

The articles were all similar in wording. However most importantly, they all ran the original suicide letter written by Yvette Mélangé, with Madame Charbonneau's name blacked out, of course.

They brought in experts to examine the note. All agreed it was consistent with the paper and ink Madame Mélangé always used, of which they found a large supply in her bedroom. As well, they all confirmed the writing to be the handwriting of the deceased and the second note to be a forgery.

The gossip about Jonathan stopped, extinguishing the flame, and the smoke blew away, revealing a clear sky.

Only Winnie understood this was not the end of it, actually it was the beginning.

Twenty-Four

My Life is here

It was a season of growth. The weeds in the fields were taller, the goats were stouter little William was losing his baby fat; he began to look more like a child. Her friendships at church multiplied, her relationship with Celene was closer. Best of all, her feelings for Phillip grew as his for her. It grew stronger with each passing day. Would it never stop? Perhaps not, some things are everlasting, love is one of them.

It was no secret to anyone, although it went unspoken. There was a future for Jolene and Philip.

It was on one of their picnics, as William slept at their feet, Philip reached out, taking Jolene's hand.

"Jolene, I have something to ask you. I think you know what I'm going to say."

She silently waited, smiling.

"Jolene, I love you so much. I can't picture my life without you. I'm asking you to be my wife."

Jolene was shaking, smiling, and nearly crying.

"I love you, too, Philip. I so much want to say yes; my heart tells me so, only my mind says different. This is who I am, yet, you don't know who I was. My past is like a ship with a hole in its side. It will sail just fine, but it's taking in water little by little. In time it will stall and sink."

"Holes can be mended," Philip added.

Jolene let out a long sigh. "Let me tell you my story. If you still feel no different, I'll marry you."

Jolene continued to tell her tale, every gruesome detail, leaving not a single incident out, no stone unturned. It was difficult to relive those moments. Still, she wanted no secrets between them.

When she finished, she was in tears, feeling drained and ashamed. He reached out to her.

"Why would you think any of what you said would change my mind? If anything, it confirms what my heart told me, all along. You've traveled many hard roads, but none of them were of your own choosing. These weren't choices, these were misfortunes. It only makes me prouder of you, a woman that stood up for her beliefs despite the cruel circumstances."

At that moment, William woke. His first action was to rise on all fours, charging them. It was just the thing to break the serious mood, as they laughed, both of them fussing over the child, as he crawled over them.

"This is another reason; I feel I need to explain."

Philip looked at her confused.

"It's about William, I haven't been completely honest."

She continued to tell the whole story of Winnie, Jonathan, and little William's true identity.

When she finished, Philip looked at her in shock. "I don't understand. How could a woman do that to her husband and her own flesh and blood?"

"She thinks she's doing right," Jolene answered, sounding sympathetic.

"I'm sorry, I don't buy it. A child belongs with his mother. No child should be denied a mother's love. And to hide your true self to the world is a sin. *This above all: to thine own self be true!* But, worst of all is to deceive your husband; to lie to the man God made you one with...that is the greatest sin of all."

There was a moment a look of understanding moved between Jolene and Philip.

"So, when they call for William, will you go, too?"

"I will only go to deliver William to his mother, after doing that I will return. My life is here, now, here with you."

Twenty-Five

An Interesting Hypothesis

After the success of the Pinkerton Agency, the Private Investigator became all the rage, especially when states allowed an agent's testimony to stand in court. Of course, only the wealthy benefited from such services. Poor folk settle their differences with a punch or a gunshot; only rich folk take their foes to court, to run them over hot coals. A court judgment could ruin a person's life far worse than a physical beating or gunfire could ever.

No one was safe, unfaithful husbands and wives, seedy landlords, conniving business partners, competition in commerce and, of course, politics.

In New Orleans, the most sort after was the Addison Agency. Bernard Addison was once a Pinkerton man, he saw the writing on the wall, and followed the money.

Madame Charbonneau, like most of Addison's clients, it appalled her that his office was on Bourbon Street. She purposely hired a closed-in cab to take her there; she wore a black veil across her face when entering and exiting the building.

"Madame Charbonneau, please, take a seat," Addison stood, gesturing to the chairs in front of his desk.

"I hope you have some good news for me, today," Madame said, taking a seat, removing the veil from her face.

Addison took his seat. "I have news for you, Madame, if it is good news or bad, that is for you to decide."

"Go ahead, I'm listening," she said.

Addison put some sheets of paper in order on his desk, and then continued to make his report.

"We've done what you've asked, Madame, and more. As you know, I have a good-sized staff. Even so, I headed most of these investigations personally. We followed Judge Gibbs closely, only to come up with nothing. The man is honest as the day is long. Interesting note, since he's cleared of any infidelities to his wife, he refuses to be alone in a room with a woman. If he has a meeting with a woman, he makes sure there's another person in the room, preferably a man. I don't blame him, to be honest. I think this is a smart move.

"His wife, on the other hand, is a bundle of mystery and intrigue. She is as deceitful as her husband is straightforward."

Addison picked up a sheet of paper, handing it to Madame; it was a hand drawn map of New Orleans and its surrounding areas.

"As you see on this map, I've circled an area not far from the edge of the city. It's a cottage, owned by the Gibbs. I followed Mrs. Gibbs to the cottage; I saw some strange goings-on.

"A colored woman and her child inhabit the cottage. The boy's not more than a year old. At least, that's how it appeared to me, at the first. Then something most bizarre happened. The colored woman who lives there went off with a colored man, while Mrs. Gibbs spent the entire day alone with the baby. I managed to move in closer to observe. Mrs. Gibbs not only played with the child, she showered it with affection.

"Later when the colored couple returned, Mrs. Gibbs left, but not before she hugged and kissed the child, driving away with tears in her eyes.

"It was all too out of the ordinary. I have a theory that may explain the truth behind this oddity. Would you like to hear it?"

"That's what I pay you for, isn't it?" Madame remarked coldly.

"Well, my theory is this. If you remember Mrs. Gibbs was pregnant. Sadly, the child was stillborn. Except I believe the child didn't actually die. She had had an affair with a colored man, and had his baby. She said it was stillborn, immediately buried it, so her husband would never find out the truth, thinking his child was dead and buried.

"Of course, the child was black like the father, so she had to dispose of it. I think Mrs. Gibbs bought the cottage, having one of her servants move in to care for the child. She visits the child whenever she can, keeping it a secret from her husband and the world."

Addison sat, smiling, waiting for Madame's compliments on his genius, which she never acknowledged.

"That's an interesting hypothesis you have, Mr. Addison." She stood up to leave. "I'll be in touch."

"Good day, Mrs. Gibbs."

Before leaving the building, she placed the veil across her face. Sitting in the dark of her carriage, Madame smiled with the satisfaction of knowing the truth. It wasn't the father that was black, it was the mother.

Twenty-Six

Gone

The day finally came; there was a felling of joy and celebration in the air. Jolene spent the morning, washing and grooming, little William as well. She dressed the boy in his Sunday best. As for her, Jolene wore a dress designed and sown by many of the women of the parish. She was so pleased with it. She'd never owned anything so lovely in her life.

Philip promised her it would be a day of surprises. The first surprise was when two carriages pulled up to the back of the cottage. One was a broken-down old one-horse wagon. The driver was Celene, in the back sat some of the women from the church. The other was a carriage, driven by one of the young men of the church. They'd decorated it with flowers. Even the horse wore flowers around its neck.

The women jumped from the wagon, gathering around Jolene, laughing and chattering.

"We've come to help," Celene announced for all. "First, we will take William with us. You can't marry with a baby on your hip." They all laughed. Then Celene pointed to the carriage. "And this will take you to the church, just like a princess in a fairytale."

"It's beautiful. Where did Philip get it?" Jolene asked.

"Oh, he has friends," Celene smiled.

For the next few minutes the women primped and fussed over her, making sure everything was just right.

"Enough of this; it's time to go," Celene announced.

Jolene looked on uneasily, as one of the women took up little William.

"Don't worry, we've all had children. We know what we're doing," one of the women interrupted Jolene, as she listed all the things needed to care for William.

Jolene handed over a bag of William's things she prepared the night before, in foresight.

"Now, get going to the church, before my brother changes his mind," Celene joked.

The wagon carrying Celene, the women, and William, rode behind the carriage carrying Jolene, across the field, through town, and to the church.

There was a large group of parishioners standing, waiting outside the church. They applauded when she arrived. They continued cheering as she entered the church, after which they entered.

Flowers were everywhere; the scent was sweet, filling the air, filling the church. No one would ever imagine it had once been a barn.

Off in the corner, young Henry Lyte sang *Abide with me*. The dear boy's voice had not changed as of yet. His angelic round notes floated to heaven, echoing back to fill the church.

> *I fear no foe, with Thee at hand to bless*
> *Ills have no weight, and tears no bitterness*
> *Where is death's sting? Where, grave, thy victory?*
> *I triumph still, if Thou abide with me.*

Jolene waited in the back of the church, as everyone took a seat.

Old man Driscoll escorted Jolene down the isle. Jolene asked him to do the honors, as he was the oldest man in the church, one of the elders, and well liked and respected. How old, no one knew, not even he knew.

Philip stood nervously waiting at the front of the church, alongside Reverend Miner, pastor of *Flock of the Good Shepherd Church*, in the next county, a full day's ride away.

Jolene's mind was spinning, her knees went weak, her mouth was dry, and her hands were shaking. It wasn't till old man Driscoll took her to the front; taking her hand and offering it to Philip did she believe she could get through it all without fainting.

Philip took hold of her hand; it was then she realized he was just as nervous, perhaps more so.

She tried to pay attention to the ceremony; she understood its importance, only it was no use. Her mind was elsewhere, the past, present and future flashing before her. It wasn't until the Reverend Minor said, "You may now kiss the bride," and the congregation cheered then she came back down to earth.

Afterwards, there was a reception behind the church. All the people wished the couple well. There were no wedding gifts given. Philip asked that there be none. These were poor folk, and he didn't want a burden placed on them, only that they share in the celebration.

There wasn't one person, young or old that didn't give Jolene a hug. She could hardly contain her joy. Looking about, now, she felt at home. She watched Philip move about the crowd. She realized one reason she loved him so was because of the love others had for him, the true measure of your love and worth.

Jolene walked about with William in her arms. She never spent a moment away from the child since they first arrived at the cottage. She felt guilty at the thought of leaving him with someone else for the night.

"Don't you worry, he'll be just fine. I'll take care of him like he was my own," Celene assured Jolene as she took William from her. William was use to Celene, he didn't make a fuss. "Besides, it's only for one night," Celene added.

All concerned decided Celene would care for William at Jolene's home. It would make things easier and less strange for the child. Jolene watched as Celene and William moved away. She remained lost in thought, until Philip came up behind her, wrapping his arms around her.

"You ready, Mrs. Anderson?"

She smiled at being called Mrs. Anderson for the first time; she liked the sound of it.

The people cheered, throwing rice, as they drove away in the carriage she arrived in. Jolene held no idea where he was taking her for their honeymoon night. It didn't matter to her, as long as she was with him, she trusted him.

****

Cynthia Rawson had the sweetest log cabin on the edge of Sans Non. Her husband, Dundy, built it as his wedding gift to her. That was more than forty-eight years ago. Dundy passed on six years before. She never remarried.

Cynthia was wise with the knowledge that many years offer and a well respected woman of the church. When she learned the pastor and Jolene were to marry, it moved her heart. She put forward her home for their wedding night; she would stay with friends.

Jolene was moved to tears when they entered the cabin. There was a warm, glowing blaze in the hearth, lighting up the one-room cabin. The congregation placed flowers everywhere, filling the room with fragrance. There were rose peddles sprawled atop the bed.

Philip took her in his arms, kissing her. Nothing ever felt so right to her.

"Why are you crying?" he asked, smiling at her.

"I'm just so happy. I love you, Philip. I'm going to try to make you happy."

"You already have."

It was strange to think this was a new experience for Jolene; everything was changed in her life and mind. Everything that once caused her sorrow, now, gave her joy. What once filled her with fear now filled her with hope. Now, there was love.

In the past, men were something to avoid. They brought grief and trouble. Except now, there was Philip. Everything was different with him.

In the past, nakedness was uncomfortable. It brought embarrassment and awkwardness, although now there was Philip. Intimacy was something never given, always taken. Yet now, there was Philip. Now, there was love.

****

The morning light poured over the bed like honey. Jolene's eyes fluttered from the brightness of the sun's rays. She found herself cradled in Philips strong arms. She took in a deep breath, taking in the scent of him, hearing his heartbeat echoing in her ear, as she rested on his chest.

She rose up, placing her lips on his, gently waking him with a kiss. Without opening his eyes, he held her tighter, a growing smile beaming across his face.

"Morning, Mr. Anderson," she whispered.

"Morning, Mrs. Anderson," he replied.

They rolled over laughing.

"We need to get going," she added.

Philip looked across the room at the clock on the mantle.

"It's seven. I told the widow Rawson we'd be gone by ten."

"That gives us three hours," she giggled. "What should we do, Mr. Anderson?"

"Now, let me think about that, Mrs. Anderson."

****

They both sat up front on the carriage, Jolene's arm entwined in Philip's. The sound of the goats bleating grew louder as they approached the cottage.

Jolene was expecting that once Celene heard the carriage approaching, she would come out to greet them, holding William. All was quiet.

"Celene…!" Jolene shouted as she jumped from the carriage, walking to the house. Philip remained outside, hobbling the horse.

"Philip…Phillip!" Jolene cried out from inside the cottage. He dropped what he was doing, rushing in.

Lying face down on the floor was Celene, a pool of blood around her head. Philip fell to his knees, turning her over. Looking over his shoulder, Jolene stood, crying into her hands. "…Oh, my God...Oh, my God…!"

Using his sleeve, he wiped the blood from his sister's face. Bending low, he placed his ear next to her face.

"She's still alive! We need to get her to a doctor." Then he looked up. "Where's William?"

Jolene ran about the house, looking in every nook and cranny, under anything and everything, shouting, "William! William!" As she searched the house, she frantically announced, "He's not here…He's not here!"

Returning, Jolene stood looking with blank sorrowful eyes down at Philip and Celene.

"He's not here…he's gone," she declared in a cold frozen tone.

There was nothing Philip could do at that moment, first things first. He took Celene up in his arms, carrying her out to the carriage.

Jolene followed him outside, watching as he placed his sister in the back. She stood near the carriage as Philip got up top.

"You go ahead," Jolene said. "I need to look around some more, maybe he's wandered off."

"I'll be at the church. When I get there, I'll have some of the men come out to help you look. I love you," was the last he said as he drove off.

Jolene ran around circling the cottage, over and over, the circle growing larger with each pass.

****

With the help of many of the men of the parish, they scanned the entire area a half-mile around the cottage, even going into the woods. When it was beginning to get dark, they gave up, vowing to start again with the first light. Each silently and secretly believing it was useless.

Jolene went to the small apartment in back of the church, where Celene and Philip lived. Celene was on her bed, her face battered and bloody, as she floated in and out of consciousness.

"Oh, Jolene, I'm so sorry," Celene murmured.

"Hush, now," Jolene said. "Save your strength."

"No, I must tell you what happened. It was late. William was sleeping. Suddenly, two large white men kicked in the door. Before I could say a word, one of them hit me. The two of them continued to hit me. That's the last I remember."

"Someone's taken William, but it's not your fault. You just get better," Jolene contended. Looking to her husband, she announced, "I need to go to William's mother. I have to tell her what's happened."

"I'll go with you," Philip said.

"No, Celene needs you," Jolene replied.

Struggling, using all her strength, Celene reached out, placing her hand on Jolene's "I'll be fine," she whimpered. "Philip's place is with you, with his wife."

****

Seated in the parlor, Winnie became aware of someone else in the room. She looked up from her book to see Ma Cherie standing in the doorway.

"You scared me," Winnie laughed. "I didn't know you were there."

Ma Cherie stood silent, nervously looking about the room, as if intentionally trying not to make eye contact.

"What's the matter?" Winnie finally had to ask.

"Ah…ah…" Ma Cherie stuttered. "Jolene's here," she said at last.

"Well, don't just stand there! Show her in!" Winnie shouted, tossing the book aside, shooting up off the sofa. She rushed passed Ma Cherie and out of the parlor to greet Jolene, an explosive smile on her face.

Leaving the room, all Winnie could see was Jolene, hardly noticing the man standing at Jolene's side. She rushed across the hall to hug her, Jolene remained motionless, and then their eyes met.

There was no smile on Jolene's face, only, a faraway sadness in her eyes that told of misfortune and disaster, a look that foretold death or worse.

Winnie stopped inches from Jolene, her smile disappeared like a sandcastle washed away by an ocean wave.

"What's wrong? Where's William?" she asked with apprehension, it being her first concern.

There was no way that Jolene could soften it. She came right out and said it. "I don't know where he is, Winnie. Someone stole him. I'm sorry."

With that, Winnie's eyes rolled back in her head. Her head tilted to the ceiling. Her body went limp, falling to the floor.

Philip picked her up in his arms, taking her to the parlor; he placed her down on the sofa. When she came to, Jolene was at her side.

"Winnie, it couldn't have been helped. Two men forcibly took him," Jolene explained.

"Who's this?" Winnie asked, gesturing to Philip.

"This Philip, he's my husband," Jolene said with a slight smile.

Winnie chuckled, "I'm glad for you."

Jolene remained silent, feeling responsible and ashamed.

"Tell me everything. I want to hear everything you know," Winnie asked. There was a far-off look on Winnie's face and in her eyes, as if she already knew what to expect, there were no surprises.

Jolene spent the next few minutes telling Winnie every detail of the past two days. She told her about the wedding, and that they left William in good hands. She told of when they returned to find Celene beaten nearly to death by two strangers, how they searched for hours for William to no avail.

"Winnie, I'm so sorry. Please, forgive me," Jolene pleaded in tears.

Winnie sat up, taking Jolene's hand. "There is nothing to forgive. I know what happened. Even guarded by a squad of soldiers, this still would have occurred, for I know who did this, as well as why they did this."

"Who...?" Jolene asked.

"It's best you don't know. I don't want you involved." Winnie rose from the sofa, walked to Philip, reaching up to kiss his check. "Congratulation, you've got yourself a fine woman."

"I think so," Philip answered, smiling.

"Treat her good. Make her happy. Lord knows she deserves it."

"I will," Philip promised.

Winnie turned to Jolene, again. "Do me one last favor. Go back to your life. The cottage is yours. Only, when I rescue William, I will deliver him to you, to stay with you for just a short time longer."

"Of course," Jolene responded humbly.

Winnie spoke loudly, as if addressing someone not present in the room, an announcement to the heavens. "I will get back my son, even if I have to kill her. You can bend a branch only so far. Eventually, it will snap."

Twenty-Seven

The Fire of Anger

"I need to speak with Madame Charbonneau," Winnie demanded, her hands clutching the bars of the front gate.

"Is Madame expecting you?" asked one of the guards.

"Just tell her Winnie is here to see her, she'll know."

Huffing and puffing, the guard walked off, entering the house, a moment later, he was back.

"Madame will see you," he said as he unlocked the gate.

Winnie pushed the guards aside, heading for the front door. One of the guards rushed forward, working his way ahead of her.

The guard escorted her into the house and down the hall. Before he could knock on the office door, Winnie pushed him aside, crashing through.

"I'm sorry, Madame," the guard apologized, standing behind Winnie.

"It's all right," Madame said. "You may leave. I can handle her."

Once the guard left, closing the door, Winnie jumped forward, screaming at Madame. "Where is he?"

"He...?" Madame asked mockingly. "Whom are you talking about?"

"Don't play games with me! Where do you have my son?"

"Son...? You have a son? I didn't know you had a son. Congratulations."

Winnie felt she was about to lose control. As angry as she was, she was aware that her bull in the china shop approach would only work against her. She stopped for a moment, took in a deep breath, releasing it slowly before continuing.

"Please, I don't want to fight. We both know what's happening. Is it money? What is it you want?"

"Very well, let's talk," Madame agreed. "Please, sit down."

Winnie ignored the gesture, continuing to stand.

"I said 'sit down'!" Madame shouted angrily, sending a fearful chill all through Winnie; she sat down.

Madame calmed, speaking softly, firmly, in a matter-of-fact tone. "Yes, I have your son. I'm not going to tell you where, nor will I give him up. Not easily, that is.

"I'm sure you'll be glad to know your husband reads like a book, he's exceptionally upright. I couldn't dig up any dirt on him, whereas, you are a cornucopia of misfortune and lies. I could ruin yours and your husband's lives in a single afternoon."

"Why are you doing this?" Winnie begged for an answer.

Madame smiled an evil smile. "Of course, there's the money as well as the power. However, one reason is I hate you and I hate your kind. To see such an inferior person do so well for herself makes me sick. I fought and struggled for everything in my life, fighting battle after battle, winning ground slowly. You marry, say 'I do' and all your sins are washed away. That's why I get such pleasure in making your life as miserable as possible." Madame ended with a slight laugh.

The fire of anger in Winnie was at full blaze, growing with each breath she took, quickly building. She could no longer hold back her feelings. She leaned forward, bent low, and with one quick swoop of her arm, she cleared Madame's desk of everything that was on it, sending books, pens, ink, and paper flying across the room.

"Damn it! Where is my son?" Winnie shouted, jumping over the desk, pouncing on top of Madame Charbonneau.

Hearing the ruckus, two security guards rushed into the house, down the hall, kicking the door open and into the office.

At first glance, it seemed as if the room was empty. Then they heard the commotion coming from behind the desk, on the floor. They dashed behind the desk to find Madame flat on her back with Winnie atop her, strangling her.

The guards each took one of Winnie's arms, lifting her off Madame. Winnie fought them, biting and kicking, until one of them, slapped her so hard she slammed into the wall.

The other guard helped Madame to her feet. She ungratefully pushed him away, as she rubbed the soreness from her throat. The two guards took hold of Winnie.

"What do you want us to do with her?" the guard asked.

Madame took a moment to gain composure, and then she took her seat, again, at her desk.

"Nothing," Madame answered, surprising everyone. She looked to Winnie. "I could have you killed; you know that, and your son, as well, except that would be too easy, and not profitable. Besides, I have a plan, and your going to dance to my tune, like it or not."

"Damn you," Winnie growled through her teeth.

"Too late, my dear, I'm already there." She looked to the guards. "Show Mrs. Gibbs out; she's apparently under stress. Obviously, she's not feeling well."

The two guards, holding Winnie's arms, started for the door.

"This is far from over," Winnie shouted as they dragged her down the hallway. "I would do anything for my son. He is my life. If anything were to happen to him, I would have no life. And a person who has not life has nothing to live for; they are the most dangerous people on the earth. You will regret the day you crossed me. I swear."

"I will be in touch," Madame shouted back frigidly.

The guards pulled Winnie out of the house, shoving her out the front gate, off the property.

****

"He's so cute," one of the girls said as they all giggled, passing William around like he was a rag doll. With all the attention the child cooed, laughed, smiled, and winning their hearts.

Madame Charbonneau's school for Fancy Girls could house and teach as many as twelve girls at a time. Now, admissions were down to only five. Of course, that could change any day with a visit from Samuel Runt.

"Oh, he's so precious," another girl announced as she cuddled William.

Headmistress, Cora, entered the room.

"Right, he's precious, now, while he's feed, clean, and he ain't fussin'. He's not so precious when it's time for feeding or he needs a bath, or he's plum tuckered out and ready to sleep, and definitely not when he needs changing."

They all remained hushed, knowing it was true.

"Y'all better start puttin' in a little more effort. I'm not gonna take care of this here baby all on my own," Cora warned.

"I'm here to become a Fancy, not a nursemaid," one of the girls protested.

"You're here to do what I tell ya," Cora shouted. "Just remember, a wealthy gentleman will pay the same for a Fancy Girl if she has either ten or nine toes, it don't matter, the price is the same."

Twenty-Eight

The Blade of the Shovel

"Come in," Jonathan reacted to the knock on his office door. He looked up to see who it was. "Addison, Barnard Addison, I haven't seen you in years. Sit down...sit down." The two men reached across Jonathan's desk to shake hands, and then Addison sat down. "So, Barnard, how's the private investigation business?"

"That's what I came to talk to you about," Addison said solemnly. His serious tone erased the smile from Jonathan's face.

"This sounds serious."

"It is, as far as I'm concerned. You have a few minutes?"

"Yes, of course."

"You've always treated me fair, Jonathan; I never forgot that you've done some favors for me, I could never repay you. How long have we known each other, Jonathan?"

"I don't know, give or take five, six, years."

"Then you know what kind of man I am. I like money as much as the next person, but I do have my limits; I draw the line at some point. Well, I feel we're friends, so, I can tell you straight. I received payment to investigate you and your wife."

Jonathan sat with a shocked look on his face.

"I'll tell it all, except you've got to promise it never leaves this room. If word gets out I turned on a client, I'll lose my business."

"I promise," Jonathan agreed, leaning forward to catch every word.

"First we tailed you. You'll be glad to know we found nothing unusual about your behavior. It is your wife that gives me pause."

This caught Jonathan's full attention.

Addison continued. "Do you know your wife owns some property on the outskirts of the city, and there's a cottage on that property?"

"My wife is free to do with her money as she pleases," Jonathan answered, sounding defensive, although inwardly it bothered him Winnie never mentioned something so important to him.

Addison must have known what Jonathan was thinking.

"Yes, nevertheless, don't you think not telling you about such major purchases are somewhat out of the ordinary?"

Jonathan held no answer for this.

"There's a woman living at the cottage, a colored woman. She's living there with a child, less than a year old...a colored child. At first, I assumed the child was hers, until your wife showed up."

"What are you trying to imply?" Jonathan asked.

"I'm not implying anything, my friend. Only, that I do have my suspicions. When your wife visited the cottage, the colored woman left, leaving your wife alone with the child. For the entire day, she not only played with the child, she showered him with signs of affection."

"So, she's an emotionally caring woman," Jonathan pointed out, again, sounding defensive.

"Jonathan, listen to what you're saying. Caring for a slave is one thing; to spend an entire day mollycoddling a colored baby is just too suspicious."

"Then tell me what your suspicions are."

"Jonathan, understand this is all speculation. I will never discuss this with anyone other than you. I hope I'm wrong for your sake.

"I don't want to dwell on the recent loss of your child. I'm sure that hurt you beyond measure. You know that far better than I. What if... just suppose...the child didn't die? What if it was a colored baby? Perhaps, she had an affair with a colored man, and this was his child not yours. She'd want to keep the truth from you at any cost. So, she bought the cottage, and set up a woman to raise the child. And she tells you the baby died at childbirth. I know it sounds far-fetched, nevertheless these things do happen."

"I don't believe it! I can't believe it!" Jonathan said, shaking his head.

Addison handed a slip of paper to Jonathan.

"This will show you where the cottage is. Perhaps, you can sort this all out. I do hope I'm wrong."

Jonathan looked at the map, quickly folding it back up again, placing it in his top pocket.

"Who hired you for the investigation?" Jonathan asked.

"I'd rather not say," Addison responded. "I told you it could damage my reputation."

"I've already promised to never mention this to anyone, not even my wife. So, tell me who hired you."

Addison took a long moment to answer. "It was Madame Charbonneau."

****

Ma Cherie couldn't help notice that neither Winnie nor Jonathan so much as touched their dinner, as she took away the plates.

"Master Jonathan, my cookin', was it not to your liking?" Ma Cherie asked, walking backward toward the kitchen, examining the plates.

"It was just fine, Ma Cherie, I'm just too tired to eat."

Ma Cherie looked at Winnie.

"I'm just not hungry, tonight, Ma Cherie. Thank you, it was delicious."

Ma Cherie entered the kitchen, sure something was wrong.

Winnie and Jonathan sat silently, wearing long faces, as if both of them were carrying the weight of the world.

"Do you still love me?" Winnie asked in a whisper, avoiding eye contact.

"Strange," he said, "I was just about to ask you the same question."

She reached out, placing her hand on his. "Of course, I love you. Why would you ask such a question?"

"Why would you?" he questioned back.

Neither one found the courage to answer.

****

The full moon illuminated the entire world, starting with their bedroom. Carefully and gently Jonathan got out of bed. After putting on his robe and slippers, he quietly left the room. He tiptoed down the stairs, descending slowly to minimize the squeaking of the wooden stairs under his feet. Little by little, he opened the backdoor, the rusty hinges whining.

It was easy to navigate under the light of the full moon. He found the shovel he told the gardener to leave on the side of the house.

He walked to the far back end of the property, to the large maple tree. In the silver moonlight, he found the outline of the small grave without difficulty. It wasn't so long ago, yet not quite lost in the cover of grass.

Somehow, deep inside, it felt like committing sacrilege. Still, he pressed on, putting the blade of the shovel over the heart of the grave, placing his foot on the scoop, pressing down. The steel cut through the top soil like a knife cutting bread. After that, the soil was dense, needing more force.

Finally, when he was nearly four feet down, he broke down crying, falling to his knees. This was an empty grave. Somewhere out there in the night, his son was still alive. And what made it worse, his wife, the love of his life, had lied to him.

Twenty-Nine

Revelations, Confessions, Admissions

With as much care as they could muster, they moved Celene from the small apartment in the back of the church to the cottage, where Jolene and Philip could care for her till she recovered.

The swollen bruises on her face were beginning to heal. Still, it would take a long time before she was well and strong enough to be on her own.

Despite Celene's protest over all the fuss, Jolene insisted on caring for her as a nurse would, washing her, feeding her, and reading to her at night. It wasn't till late in the evening Jolene was able to sit and relax with her husband.

"You're an amazing woman, Mrs. Anderson," Philip declared, wrapping his arm around her.

"I don't feel so amazing," she sobbed. "In fact, I feel the opposite. I feel so helpless, so hopeless. I can't help feeling this is all my fault, and I can't think of a way to fix it."

Philip took both her hands, moving his face inches from hers. "Jolene, look at me. None of this was your fault. If anyone is to blame, it's Winnie. She unfairly asked you to do everything for her son, other than give birth to him. Her place was with her son, not you. She lies to her husband, which is as bad as any infidelity. You've done everything possible, more than any friend should be asked to do."

"Poor William, I'm so afraid for him, Philip; I love that little boy."

"I know you do, Jolene, but that doesn't make it your fault."

"I wish there was something I could do," she said, falling into his arms, weeping.

"There, there…"

"And your poor sister, she was beaten for watching William, while I was off having fun. She was where I should have been. It should have been me that was beaten."

"That's not true," said a voice from across the room.

They turned to see Celene standing in the bedroom doorway.

"Celene, what are doing out of bed?" Jolene cried out, running across the room to her.

When they were face-to-face, Celene looked at her squarely. "That's not true," she repeated. "There was no way you could have prevented what happened. You weren't just having fun, you were getting married and enjoying your wedding night, which is the way it should be. Don't you dare feel guilty about anything that happened. It wasn't your fault. Philip is my brother, you are his wife, now, that makes you my sister. Don't do this to yourself."

The two women hugged, holding onto each other for a long time, crying.

"Thank you, Celene," Jolene said softly. "Come now; let's get you back into bed."

Jolene gently and slowly walked Celene into the bedroom. Getting her in bed, she tucked her in.

"God bless you," Celene whispered up. "I love you."

"I love you, too," Jolene said, bending low, kissing Celene on her cheek.

When she left the bedroom, she found Philip standing, waiting for her.

"I couldn't have said it any better," Philip said, reaching out to Jolene.

She ran into his arms, sobbing.

"Oh, Philip, you must be strong, now, for both of us."

"I'm here for you, always," he whispered in her ear. "And if I'm strong, it is because of you."

****

Winnie wasn't well. It was as plain as day. A dark cloud hovered over her, always; death's shadow clung to her like a skin she couldn't shed. Her eyes seemed focused on a place beyond the horizon, beyond sight or reach. It was noticeable to all how much weight she had lost. She looked emaciated, her cheeks sunk into the sides of her face, her luxurious hair became thin like straw, and her once glamorous looks were now fading. She became a poor facsimile of her true self.

Other than Jolene, the two people in the world who cared and loved her the most were Jonathan and Ma Cherie. Both not only worried for her, they voiced their concern many times, never stopping. Only, Winnie heard none of it. It all fell on deaf ears. Grief, worry, shame, and guilt weighed on her like a sand dune, which covered her passed her ears, blocking all outside sounds.

The worst part of it all, it was like a wedge hammered into the crevice of their marriage, becoming a chasm, which fell off into an abyss.

****

Each day, after Jonathan left for work, Winnie would sit alone with her sorrow in the parlor. With the hours passing slowly akin to drips of water little by little trying to fill an ocean.

127

"There's a woman here to see you, Winnie," Ma Cherie announced, standing in the doorway.

Winnie looked up. "Who is it?" she asked hazily.

"It's a black woman. Ain't never seen her before, says her name is Cora."

Winnie unexpectedly became alert, as if someone threw cold water on her.

"Show her in, and leave us alone," she ordered.

A moment later, Cora entered; Ma Cherie closed the parlor door.

****

Ma Cherie walked to the kitchen, purposely treading heavily to make it seem she left them alone, and then she tiptoed back to the parlor door. Gently, she placed her ear to the door.

"Cora, I never thought I'd ever see you again," Winnie said with a slight laughter of cynicism.

"What…no friendly hello?" Cora asked with the same sharpness.

"We were never friends, Cora, and you know it."

"I suppose you're right. To be honest, I never thought I'd see you again either," Cora replied coldly.

"So, why are you here?"

"Madame Charbonneau thought it best not to have direct contact with you, which is why she sent me."

"How is my son, William?"

"Oh, he's living like a little prince, all those beautiful women fussin' over him."

"Then he *is* at the school?"

Cora laughed. "I could lie to you, only, what for? Yeah, he's at the school. Remember, we've got guards everywhere, big brutes, too. It would take an army to get to your son."

"I just need to know, is he well?"

"He's as well as can be," Cora answered.

"What does Madame want?"

"What does Madame always want? If it's not power, it's money."

"How much of each does she want for my William?"

"She wrote it down on a slip of paper, here."

A moment passed, as Winnie read the note.

"This is a dreadfully large sum," Winnie declared.

"I wouldn't know," Cora replied. "I never read it. Only, knowing Madame, I'm sure it's an edgy price."

"Edgy doesn't come close to describing the amount," Winnie assured out loud. "What if I can't come up with this amount? What if I could only come up with half?"

"Knowing Madame, I'd suspect you'd only get back half of your son."

"Do you hear what you're saying?" Winnie entreated Cora.

"It is what it is," Cora declared, sounding not in the least interested.

"Tell me something, Cora?"

"What's that?"

"How do you sleep at night? You're a black woman; don't you have any pride in your race, any compassion, any feeling of connection?"

"You're one to talk," Cora snapped back.

Cora had hit her mark, straight into Winnie's heart. What was most painful of all, Winnie knew it was true.

Cora continued, "Do I have any feelings? Of course, I do. Actually, just not now, I had those years ago. You're just asking me at the wrong time in my life. You should have asked me when I was molested by the older men of the plantation, including my uncles and family friends, not to mention the white overseers. You should have asked me when my mother gave me up for a bag of rice. You should have asked me before I married at fifteen and nearly beaten to death, or before I had three babies that they took from me and sold at auction. You got the right question, just the wrong time to ask it. I no longer feel. I don't care anything about you. I don't care if you get beaten into the ground, both you and your baby, or get to live happily every after, it makes no difference to me. I couldn't care less."

"I'm sorry," Winnie said, fully meaning it.

"You're sorry, how do you think I feel? You have one month to come up with the full sum of money."

"I may need more than a month."

"Madame doesn't care. A month is all you've got."

"How should I get the money to her?"

"I'll come to collect it. Only, let me know through the post."

"Tell Madame I'll have it ready soon."

"Good. No need to show me to the door, I'll find my own way out," Cora said.

With that, Ma Cherie rushed toward the kitchen.

Winnie stood in the parlor, her mind racing. How would she come up with that kind of money?

Ma Cherie stood in the kitchen, her mind thinking about what to do next.

****

In his own quiet way, Jonathan was suffering, as well. Winnie was the love of his life. Yet here, after talking with Addison, he held misgivings. Why had Winnie bought property on the edge of the city with a cottage on it? Who was the black woman living in the cottage? He suspected it must be Jolene. Winnie loved and trusted Jolene. It was the only person he could think of that she would entrust with a child...her child, he wondered.

Who was this small black boy, and why was Winnie visiting him to shower him with affection. It all appeared to back much of what Addison proposed. Nevertheless, he had to find out the truth for himself.

Checking with public records at City Hall and using the map Addison gave him, he learned the exact whereabouts of the cottage.

Leaving no word at his office about where he was going, he took the rest of the day off to investigate.

On horseback, at full gallop, the trip took less than a half-hour. Not far from the cottage, Jonathan dismounted, deciding to draw near on foot. He got as close as he could, while still keeping his distance to remain unseen. He heard voices; only, he was too far to make out the words.

In time, a woman came out of the house, he recognized her immediately; it was Jolene, confirming his suspicions. Then a man came out to join her, a black man, standing extraordinarily close to Jolene. It was obvious they were intimate.

Oddly, a third voice called from inside the cottage, a woman's voice. It was all too strange.

He felt tempted to walk out into the open and approach them. After all, he was the owner of the property. Why should he have to hide? He had nothing to be ashamed of.

Besides, he was a friend of Jolene; he considered himself so, and believed she did, too. Perhaps, if he was straightforward with her, they could air everything out in the open and get to the bottom of this. However, a fear of dread washed over him, forcing him to hold back. Without more information, he might be charging in the wrong direction, causing more harm than good.

Deciding he would not make a move without more inquiry, he walked back to his horse and rode back to the city.

***

Ma Cherie entered the dining room to remove the breakfast plates. As usual, Winnie only picked at her food like a bird. It hardly looked touched.

"Ma Cherie...?" Jonathan called out. "Don't you think Winnie's looking peaked, lately?" he asked, as if Winnie wasn't even in the room.

"I've been saying that for weeks, now," Ma Cherie agreed, also speaking as if it were just the two of them, she and Jonathan.

Jonathan reached into his jacket pocket, taking out his billfold, removing money from it. He placed the bills on the table, scooting them toward Winnie. She looked at the wad like it was a scorpion.

"Here, my dear; why don't you and Ma Cherie take a holiday. Go into town, do what women love to do. Do some shopping; eat at Antoine's, whatever your heart desires."

"Would you meet us at Antoine's for lunch?" Winnie asked hopefully. She wanted so much to mend the wounds hurting them.

"I can't think of anything nicer, only, I'm afraid I have a full day of work; perhaps, some other time?" He pushed the bills closer to her. "Please, it will do you good."

It was clear Winnie felt disappointed. She looked up at Ma Cherie who was smiling and nodding her head.

"Come on, Winnie, it will do ya good," Ma Cherie added.

"Very well, we will," Winnie consented wearing a half smile. Something well missed by all, especially Jonathan.

Wiping his lips with his napkin, Jonathan rose from his chair, reached over, kissing Winnie on her check.

"Well, I must be going. You two have a pleasant day."

****

It had been a long time since Winnie had a day to herself in town. She went to her room, rummaging through her closet for just the right outfit. Ma Cherie went to her room, took the hatbox out from under her bed, and removed the hat, the one with the red feather.

After Winnie and Ma Cherie left for the day, the house was quiet. It was still morning when Jonathan returned home. A strong feeling of guilt ran through his veins, not a feeling he enjoyed. He felt covered in shame. Never had he done or said anything deceitful to Winnie. Only, he needed to know the answers to the questions that would not stop haunting him, a cruel torture. He'd given up on the hope of one day his wife would break down and tell him the truth. It seemed she never would. As much as this upset him, he needed to put that behind, and find the answers for himself.

There was another issue that needed to be taken into consideration, a new element that took root in his soul, an entity taking over his mind, consuming him as a wild beast devours its prey. That creature growing in him was the green-eyed monster jealousy. It will eat at you till all that was you is gone, and what is left is not you.

What if Addison had it right? What if the child Winnie carried was not his? The grave was empty, which could only mean the child was still alive. And why would Winnie hide the truth from him?

He didn't know what he was looking for; however, he knew where he needed to look. If Winnie wanted to hide something, the only logical place would be within her most private things.

Upstairs in their bedroom, the first place he looked was in her closet. He shuffled between her dresses, checking pockets. Holding her shoes up, shaking them. He opened hatboxes, taking out the hats. There was nothing suspicious.

He sat down at her dresser, opening the drawers one by one, rummaging through them. There was nothing out of the ordinary.

He fell to his knees, bent low, looking under the bed. There was a hatbox filled with nothing other than letters.

It didn't take him long to figure it out. These were all letters to Winnie from Jolene at the cottage.

Starting with the oldest date, he read every letter. When he finished, he understood it all. Everything was clear.

He was a father, he had a son. The child was black, that was sure, and the only reason Winnie would lie to him, going through so much trouble to hide it. He also read how she believed she was doing it for the betterment of all of them, especially their son. It frustrated and confused him.

He arranged the letters to the order they were originally in, placing them back in the hatbox. They looked exactly the way he found them under the bed. Rising, moving across the room, in the corner of his eye he saw something move. It startled him, making him jump.

It relieved him to see it was nothing more than his own reflection in the full-length mirror staring back at him. He stopped for a moment, fixated on his mirror image. It looked like him, no doubt, except something was different, something had changed. He couldn't put his finger on it, not at first he couldn't, and then he realized what it was. He was looking at a dishonest man.

****

That night after dinner, Winnie and Jonathan sat in the parlor, near the fireside. The orange glow of the flames bathed over Winnie. Jonathan couldn't help staring at her, admiring her beauty, and realizing once more, as many times before, how much he loved her.

"It seemed a day out has done you good," he commented.

Winnie smiled at him.

Jonathan wasn't sure how he would word what was in his heart, still, he knew what he had to say.

"Winnie, you know I love you more than anything in this world. I want you to know I will always be there for you. There is nothing in the world that you can do, that could ever change that. We must never hide anything from each other. Our love is strong, it can withstand anything. I know that both within my heart and my soul."

It was a strange statement to make, indeed. Winnie could have easily played the game and dismissed it as so to him with a smile and a laugh. Instead, she looked at him solemnly, deciding to speak only the truth, at least as far as her predicament would allow.

"If I have been untrue, it was never to you, it would be to me. If I were to hide anything from you, know that it was never to hurt you. I've always had and will put you before me. If I ever hide anything from you, know that it will only be for a time. For in time, I will always tell you the truth. Please, always bear with me."

It was all so strange. They faced the predicament, and in their own way, in their own voice, knowing that in time they would solve it. At that moment, Jonathan decided to never press the point again. He would wait silently. He would bear with her.

Thirty

Good for the Soul

There seemed no relief for Winnie, the pressure was more than one person could handle. Desperate, she decided to seek solace where she never had before – the church.

Faith was the stronghold of so many, including Jolene and Ma Cherie. Never did they miss a Sunday church service. They never preached to her, still, they appeared having an inner peace she always was envious of.

The Basilica of Saint Louis meant so much to Winnie. It was on that very altar of the Basilica she witnessed death, illness, and eventually her marriage ceremony performed on that altar. Each time, Father Bon Coeur was there. She wondered if he ever made the connection that each time it was she. It was doubtful.

For some reason, in Winnie's mind, Father Bon Coeur represented sanctuary, salvation, forgiveness, mercy, and release. These were all the things her spirit craved. Having no idea where else to come by these things, she decided to visit the priest.

The cathedral was near empty. A tiny woman in front of the altar was mopping the marble floor.

"Excuse me; do you know where I can find Father Bon Coeur?" Winnie asks the woman.

The old woman drops her mop, the sound echoes off the wall.

"I'll see if the Father can see you?" she said walking away, her frail thin body hunched over, shuffling her feet.

"Tell him. . ." Winnie called out, except before she could finish the woman was out of earshot.

A minute later, Father Bon Coeur walked toward her, the old woman hobbling behind him.

"Mrs. Gibbs, how wonderful to see you, again," he stood, smiling, reaching out, and taking her hand to shake it.

"You remember me?" she asked.

He laughed slightly. "Of course, I do. How could I forget? It was such a lovely wedding; you were such a lovely couple. Besides, it isn't every day I perform a wedding for a judge." He gestured to the front pew. "Please, be seated."

Once seated, he turned to her, still smiling.

"So, Mrs. Gibbs, what brings you here, today?"

She wished she had a smile to reciprocate. In fact, the solemn look on her face erased the smile on his.

"I need help. I'm sorry, I didn't know who else to turn to."

"Mrs. Gibbs, there's no need to apologize, that's what I'm here for. You can tell me anything. I'll help, if I can."

"I guess you could say this is a confession."

He remained silent, listening intensely.

"To confess, do I have to tell you every detail?" she asked.

"It's hard to say. It all depends on...well, let's make a start of it, and see how far we get."

Winnie sighed deeply, and began speaking in a low whisper, afraid her voice would echo off the marble that was all around, letting the whole world hear.

"I have been living a lie. Not too long ago, an incident happened in my life that I believed would not only affect my life negatively, but also of the ones I love, including my husband. I felt the only way to combat this effect was to keep it hidden from the world. Except, as I know; now, it's gotten out of hand, one lie leads to two, so on and so on. What is worse is other issues have come into play; the outcome is not looking that it will turn out good. Please, help me, Father."

Father Bon Coeur spoke softly, calmly, clearly, and with compassion. "Mrs. Gibbs, I can tell you are a Christian, and I can see, without a doubt, you are a good kindhearted woman. However, I feel it is my responsibility to guide you in these ways. When a person confesses, they are in search of forgiveness and redemption in line with salvation. There is no salvation without redemption, and there is no redemption without forgiveness.

"In speaking our sins before God and man, we seek forgiveness, which is readily offered, but not without redemption. You tell me you've been lying to the loved ones in your life, including your husband. You show remorse, which is the first step to forgiveness; however, it's not the only step. You must do two things to complete this journey."

Winnie felt tempted to ask for the two steps, yet, waited for him to complete his thought.

"You must renounce your actions, which means you must no longer lie, you must stop at once. What else that needs doing is penance. You must make well what you have broken; make good what you have made evil. You must not only stop lying; you must tell those you lied to that you have lied. As hard as it may seem, you must confront these people with the truth, especially your husband."

Winnie remained intently looking at him before speaking. "I can't do that."

"I'm sorry," he said sternly. "Just regretting your actions will not do. If you do not stop lying and tell the truth, there is no forgiveness, no forgiveness, no redemption, and no salvation. I can do no more. I remain here for you, if you change your mind."

With that, Father Bon Coeur rose and walked away, his footsteps reverberating through the church. Exiting the door he entered from, he left, never looking back.

The old woman, trying to ring out the mop, accidentally knocked over her bucket, the unclean water spilled everywhere.

****

When she returned home, opening the door, Jonathan rushed from the parlor to her.

"Are you all right? You weren't here when I got home. No one knew where you were. I was worried."

She stood before him, her eyes welling up, her arms reaching out for him.

"Hold me, Jonathan."

He didn't move for a moment, her words taking him off guard, even frightening him. Finally, he moved forward taking her into his arms.

"Tighter," she moaned into his chest.

"Darling, what's wrong?" he asked softly, gripping her firmer.

"Just hold me, Jonathan. Tell me you'll never leave me."

"Of course, I'll never leave you. Now, tell me what this is all about."

"I can't," she replied.

It was then Jonathan understood this had something to do with their predicament, the one they lived with in silence, both afraid to speak.

He guided her up the stairs to their bedroom. There they made love without a word spoken.

Thirty-One

A Visit to the People's Bank

The problem wasn't the money. The Gibb family could easily afford the ransom Madame Charbonneau demanded. The problem was how Winnie could get the money without Jonathan knowing. She could easily withdraw medium size amounts from their bank account without much said. This was how she was able to afford to buy the cottage. A little here, a little there, putting the amount aside, not buying anything else, and saving it till she could afford the cottage.

This time was different. She hadn't much time, less than a month. Small amounts wouldn't help; she needed the full amount, and now. To take the full amount out of their bank account, that she couldn't hide from Jonathan.

Winnie thought of all the expensive items she owned. Perhaps, she could sell them. Maybe, it would be enough.

She spent an entire day rummaging through her belongings in her closet and dressers. By the end of the day, she held a full sack of her most expensive jewelry. As it was too late in the day to do anything with them, she hid the sack in the back of her closet.

The next morning after Jonathan left for City Hall, Winnie was out the door with her valuables.

She'd thought it over all nightlong. The most inconspicuous way was to go to the *People's Bank* or as some people called them a *Pawnbroker*. There she'd receive money for the merchandise with the possibility of getting them back before anyone, especially Jonathan, knew they were gone. It would be more like a loan than an out-and-out sale. This was highly unlikely; nevertheless, this was an outside chance she was willing to take.

She also decided to take the precaution of not trying to sell everything at only one place. This might create suspicion. So, she decided to visit every pawnbroker in the city.

The shopkeepers were more than glad to take on her goods. They were clearly of the highest quality. If she came back to reclaim the goods within ninety day, she would have to pay an interest. If she did not, the items would become theirs to sell at whatever price they could get. Either way, there was good money to be made.

At day's end, she'd pawned everything. She returned home before Jonathan. She hid the money under their bed in the same hatbox she hid the letters.

Winnie purposely kept some of her cheaper pieces of jewelry. These she'd wear in hopes of warding off any questions.

Except, Ma Cherie watched all of Winnie's comings and goings; this filled her with misgivings.

****

Jonathan received a message from Addison. It asked to meet him for lunch at a tavern, *The Black Rose,* down aways from City Hall. There were no other details other than he relayed it was most important they talk.

Leaving City Hall, Jonathan started in the direction of the tavern. To his surprise, he looked over to see Addison walking at his side.

Addison kept his voice low, "The more I thought about it, the more I realized it might be best we're not seen together. Take a left at the corner."

They walked on to an area from the main thoroughfare where there were few people. There they stopped to face each other.

"Addison, what's this all about?"

Addison reached into his jacket pocket. He took out a woman's brooch, handing it to Jonathan. He took hold of the pin, recognizing it immediately.

"Where did you get this?" Jonathan exclaimed.

"Recognize it…?"

"Of course, I do. It used to be my mother's. I gave to my wife as a gift on our wedding anniversary. Where did you get this? Were we robbed?"

"Yes and no," replied Addison.

"What's that suppose to mean?" Jonathan asked.

"Your wife's been pawning her jewelry at every pawnbroker in town."

"I don't understand. Why would she do that?"

"It's simple. For some reason, she needs money, a lot of it and right away. I figure she went to pawnbrokers in hopes she can buy the pieces back before you notice they're gone. Do you know why she might need a large sum of money?"

"I think I do," Jonathan remarked. "Addison, tell me, how did you find out about this?"

"I run in many different circles in this city than you do. Someone got in touch with me. The wife of the City Judge has a well-known face." He reached in his pocket again, pulling out a slip of paper, handing it to Jonathan. "Here's a list of the pawnbrokers she sold to. I figured you might want to reclaim your merchandise."

"Thanks, Addison, I owe you one."

"You owe me more than one, Judge."

Thirty-Two

At the Cottage

Celene was doing much better, healing a little each day. The swelling on her face began subsiding. Standing and moving about became easier for her. She began moving slowly about the house, eventually venturing outside. In time, she felt strong enough to help out in the kitchen.

"Sit down, I can do that. You need to stay off your feet," Jolene said when she turned to see Celene up and about, setting the table.

"Nonsense," Celene laughed. "Moving around will do me good. Besides, I can't stand both of you waiting on me hand and foot, when I could be doing something."

What harm could it do? Jolene thought, letting Celene have her way.

It would be just the two of them for lunch. Philip was out and about doing what pastors do.

The cottage was bright with the noonday sun, as they prayed grace, and ate in silence, till finally Celene spoke.

"I should be getting back to my apartment," she uttered.

"What are you saying? You're not well, yet."

"I'm well enough. I've overstayed my welcome. Besides, you two are newlyweds; you don't need your sister-in-law around."

Jolene placed her hand atop of Celene's. "Now, just stop there. You are family, you will always be welcomed. And you're not well enough till I say you are." She paused for a moment, and then spoke softly. "Besides, I need all the help I can get."

Celene placed her other hand atop of Jolene's. "You're worried about your friend and little William."

"That's all I think about. I can't stop. I feel so helpless. What's worse is it's not fair to Philip. I swore I would be a good wife to him, and so soon I've already broken my vow. All my energy is directed someplace else."

Jolene broke down in tears. Celene reached out, wrapping her arms around Jolene.

"Don't cry. Philip understands. He's a good man. He knows what you're going through. Don't worry; you'll have many good years together."

"Thank you," Jolene said, trying to hold back the tears and sniffling.

"I promise I won't talk about leaving again. In fact, I'm thinking of staying here forever."

Jolene sat up straight, staring at Celene.

"It was just a joke," Celene laughed.

They both flew into laughter.

"Come, now," Celene said. "Let's clean up. We can spend the afternoon making something wonderful for dinner to surprise Philip."

Jolene nodded, smiling.

"I love you, my dear sister."

"I love you, too."

Thirty-Three

Double the Price

Winnie wasn't going to take any chances her letter to Madame Charbonneau, telling her she had the full ransom, might be lost in the post. So, she instructed their carriage driver to deliver the letter.

"Make sure you give it to Madame Charbonneau. Don't leave it with the guards at the front gate; don't give it to any of the help. I want you to place this letter directly into Madame Charbonneau's hands," Winnie ordered the driver, stating it as clearly and as strongly as she could.

He returned an hour later, reporting he had not delivered the letter to the guards at the gate, although they told him they'd not allow him to see Madame Charbonneau. The driver insisted he deliver the letter to Madame and her only. It took some arguing on his part, eventually they brought him face-to-face with Madame.

"Then what happened?" Winnie asked.

"After I gave her the letter, the guards came to show me out. As I was leaving she told me to tell you that someone will get in touch with you, soon."

After dismissing the driver, there was nothing for Winnie to do other than wait. She waited the day away with no sign of Cora. This deeply worried her. This was understandable; this was a mother's nightmare. No matter how anxious she felt, trying to dismiss her feelings, she found it impossible.

It was the next day; there was still no sign of Cora. Winnie became frantic. It would be just like Madame Charbonneau to do something such as this, to make her wait, knowing it would make Winnie's suffering all the more harsh and deep.

On the third day, when she was at her wit's end, there was a knock at the front door. Winnie rushed to answer it before any of the household staff could respond. It was Cora. She didn't so much as enter before she announced why she was there.

"I'm here for the money." Cora declared callously.

"Where's William? Where's my son?"

"Take my word for it, he's fine. Now, give me the money," Cora replied unemotionally.

"Why should I take your word for it? When will you bring him to me? How do I know you'll keep your part of the bargain?"

Cora just laughed. "You have no say in this. You can't make any demands. Just pay the ransom. That's the only choice you have." She waited a moment, smiling directly into Winnie's face. "Just give me the money."

"I have to go get it," Winnie said, rushing up the stairs. Cora remained in the doorway.

Less than a minute later, Winnie returned with the cash she hid under the bed. She handed it to Cora.

"You tell Madame Charbonneau, if I don't have my son back safe within the next twenty-four hours, I kill her. I swear I'll kill her with my bare hands."

"Of course, you will," Cora said, laughing as she left.

****

Three day passed with no word from Madame Charbonneau. Winnie was beside herself in constant torment. She did her best to avoid Jonathan. Whenever that wasn't possible, she did her best to hide her inner turmoil.

Finally, on the fourth day, there was a knock at the front door. Like that last time, Winnie beat everyone to the front door, dismissing anyone who showed their face.

To her surprise and disillusionment, it wasn't Cora. Instead, a small boy, a sad looking little street urchin, stood at the door, holding an envelope. Before Winnie could say a word, he handed her the envelope and ran away.

She didn't bother to open it, entering the parlor, closing the door behind her so she could read it in private. Taking out the single slip of paper, she unfolded it. It was immediately noticeable there was no address or return address printed on the envelope and there was no closing signature on the letter. As well, the content was vague. This insured Winnie couldn't make a case against Madame Charbonneau.

All this time, Ma Cherie was in the dining room, spying, which was something she now did often. She tiptoed to the parlor, putting her ear to the door, that's when she heard Winnie let out a piercing cry, followed by a loud thud to the floor.

****

When Winnie came to, she found she was lying on the sofa with Ma Cherie seated at her side. Winnie still held the sheet of paper. Ma Cherie took it and read it out loud.

I received the money. Well done. Congratulations on sending the full amount and on time. In fact, you did such an excellent job of it with little effort; I suggest we double the price. You have one month.

Ma Cherie tenderly brushed the hair from Winnie's forehead. "Oh dear Lord, what a shame, after all you been through, losing all your good jewelry like that."

Winnie went wide-eyed, shocked to hear Ma Cherie's knowledge of it all. "How do you know that?"

Ma Cherie smiled. "There isn't much that goes on in this house that I don't know about. I've spent many an hour with my ear pressed up against walls and my eye hard-pressed to keyholes." Ma Cherie went serious. "Yes, my dear, I know all about your dilemma."

Winnie covered her face with her hands, sobbing. "Oh, Ma Cherie, what am I going to do?"

"Can you pay the new price?" Ma Cherie asked. "I mean, do you have the money?"

Winnie tried to wipe the tears from her eyes. "Of course, I can. That's not the point. I used my jewelry to get the money, so Jonathan wouldn't find out. If I were to take the money out of the bank, he would surely notice such a large amount missing. Surely, he'd question it. I've kept him out of this so far; I plan to keep it that way.

"The other thing is who's to say this is the end of it. If she can raise the price once, she can do it again and again. No, I have to stop her, right now."

Winnie rose from the sofa, walking to the desk against one of the windows. She opened the upper right-hand drawer, from it she pulled out one of Jonathan's revolvers.

Ma Cherie jumped to her feet. "Winnie, what are you thinking of doing?"

Winnie held the gun up to the light to inspect it; she then turned to Ma Cherie. "Someone needs to stop that woman. I want my son back, even if it means I blast my way in to get him. And if Jonathan finds out in the process, well then, so be it. I want my son!"

"You won't even get through the front gate," Ma Cherie pointed out.

That was a problem, making Winnie reflect on her plan a little deeper.

"I believe I know a way into the grounds and building," Winnie stated aloud.

"You do?" Ma Cherie said, smiling. "Well then, I'm going with you."

"Oh, no you don't. It's too dangerous," Winnie warned.

Ma Cheri sat down, wearing a serious look. "You know I have no family. I'm the last of it, alone in the world. I never married; I never had children. You and Jolene are the closest thing to a family I will ever have. Don't forget, I helped bring William into the world. He's as much my flesh and blood as you and Jolene are. There's no way in hell you're going to stop me from saving my family."

Winnie stood silent for the longest time, thinking.

"All right," she said, finally agreeing. "My plan's going to take money. It's extremely possible Jonathan will find out, once he discovers I've taken such a large sum out of the bank. Still, once Madame is out of the way, and I have my son, for that I'm willing to take the risk."

"So, if your husband will possibly find out, why not tell him, now? Be honest with him for once," Ma Cherie advised.

"No, there's still the outside chance he may never learn of this."

"That's if we succeed," Ma Cherie added. She continued, "You know I love you, Winnie. But, I have to say, I think you're one of the most foolhardy woman I've ever known."

Thirty-Four

A Quick Delivery

It seems an oddity that Samuel Runt enters our story again. For the moment, he will be our main focus.

If you remember, Runt was that despicable creature on the lowest rung of humanity, making his living in the slave trade. His was a specialized field, one-on-one with his clients, selling the so-called highest quality slaves to the highest bidder. When it came to Fancy Girls, Madame Charbonneau was one of his best customers.

His fame in the slave trade not only caused his business to skyrocket. It also made him a popular person in the trade and easy to find. Incidentally, or miraculously, whichever you prefer, Runt was in New Orleans in a suite at the Andrew Jackson Hotel during the time of our story.

Runt recently completed a slave delivery, a top-notch cook, to the Waller family. It was a big moneymaker, not like the sale of a young husky black man, and especially not as much as what he received for a Fancy Girl. Still, the profit was enough for a trip to New Orleans.

As always, after every transaction, Runt would dismiss his bodyguards until further notice. He was alone in his hotel room, when there was a knock at the door.

"Come in," Runt shouted at the door, thinking it was the porter come to take his luggage downstairs. You could imagine his surprise, when Winnie and Ma Cherie entered.

He half smiled, half laughed, as he recognized Winnie immediately.

"I know you," he said, pointing at Winnie. "Damned if I can remember your name. However, I remember your face. I sold you to Madame Charbonneau to become a Fancy. You seemed to have done well for yourself. If you've come to thank me for all your good fortune, there's no need."

Winnie laughed out loud. "No, I'm here to make you a proposition."

"For money, I assume," he countered.

"Yes, for money."

"Then continue, I'm all ears, and they're all yours, Madam."

"You have access to Madame Charbonneau's school. I want you to get us onto the property."

"To do what?" he asked.

"That's my business."

"I see," he responded, not sounding too keen on her answer. "You realize Madame Charbonneau is one of my most valued customers. If I were to do anything against her, I'd be sure to lose her business. That's something I wouldn't do for any price."

"She'll never know you had anything to do with it. All I want you to do is get us onto the property, get us passed the guards at the front gate. We'll do the rest. You could leave immediately. The apes that guard the front gate couldn't put two and two together if their lives depended on it."

"So, how do I help you onto the property without letting my identity known?"

"I have a plan, which I'll tell when and if you agree to my proposition."

"So how much money are you offering for my services?" he asked, plainly more interested in the money than the risk.

Winnie reached into her purse, taking out a large wad of cash. Before disclosing the amount, it was obviously large, Runt appeared to be satisfied. Winnie withdrew it early from the family bank account. Of course, there was no problem with the transaction. The bank knew her, and understood she was free to take out any portion.

However, the problem wasn't with the bank it was with Winnie. The weight of what she was doing was like a boulder the size of a house. And like the sales of her jewelry to the pawnbrokers, she held the belief she might recover the amount before Jonathan learned of any of it missing. This was a lie she told herself so often she believed it. Although, in the back of her mind she knew it was a fallacy she had made up for her inner well-being.

Ma Cherie was different. There were no blinders on her eyes. She knew from the start that sooner or later light dispels all darkness.

Finally, Runt counted the bills. "You're most generous. I'd be a fool to turn you down. So, tell me what your plan is?"

"I just want you to get us passed the front gate and into the building. Tell them you're delivering two new slave girls."

"The guards know me," Runt explained.

"Don't worry; there won't be any witnesses after we're through."

Winnie assured Runt by showing the grip of her pistol hidden in her purse. It was all a bluff, off course, yet, it did work. Runt smiled reassuringly.

"I don't want to sound ill-mannered; honestly, do you think Madame would consider this woman a candidate to be a Fancy?" His gesture to Ma Cherie was the finishing touch of his question.

Ma Cherie stepped forward. "I understand, sir. I know I'm not the Fancy Girl type. Perhaps, if you told them I'm the new cook?"

Runt smiled - an oddity for him. "I suppose that will work. Other than that, you both are too finely dressed to be slaves from a plantation. You need to go home and dress the part, something less becoming."

Both Winnie and Ma Cherie nodded, agreeing.

"So, when can we do this?" Winnie asked.

"Today?" he said, the statement sending chills through both women.

"…why not? Now is as good as ever."

Winnie reached out, taking the wad of cash from Runt.

"I'll just hold onto this until we return in different clothing. We'll be back within an hour," she said, placing the bills in her purse, turning to leave.

"I'll be waiting with anticipation, Madam."

****

Back at the Gibbs' house, Winnie and Ma Cherie fumbled through their wardrobes, selecting their oldest worn-out dresses.

It seemed far-fetched that a slave girl would own a purse, so they each put on kitchen aprons with deep pockets where they could hide the money and weapons.

"You realize this is madness, don't you?" Ma Cherie claimed as she placed her revolver in her apron pocket.

Winnie didn't answer. She knew any discussion would be futile.

Ma Cherie took hold of Winnie's hand, speaking softly and seriously. "Listen to me. What we're about to do may be morally right; however, it's not legally right. It is against the law. No matter what the outcome, we need to leave the city. If we get separated, go to the cottage. If we get William back or not, go to the cottage. I'll take care of Madame Charbonneau, you go looking for William. Remember, no matter what the outcome, head for the cottage."

"It's not too late to back out," Winnie warned.

"If I didn't want to do this, I wouldn't have agreed in the first place," Ma Cherie replied. "Come on, now. Let's go get your son."

****

Never one to squander a penny, Runt left at checkout time, rather than pay for another day for a room. They found him waiting outside the hotel, his luggage at his feet. He looked them both up and down, approvingly.

"Very good, you both look hideous," he laughed.

Winnie ignored the statement, pressing on. "So, what do we do first, hire a cab?" she suggested.

"What we do first, my lady, is pay for services rendered," Runt said, positioning himself before Winnie, his hands flapping behind his back, demanding payment. Winnie reached into one of the pockets of her apron, handing him the wad of cash. In a blink, he stuffed the bills in his pocket. With her other hand, again, she exposed for only a moment, the pistol in her other pocket, to insure Runt would not try to do anything contrary to the plan.

Runt smiled, nodding affirmatively. "Now we hire a cab, of which you will be paying for."

The cabby placed Runt's luggage in the back of the cab, only helping Runt into the carriage, not Winnie or Ma Cherie.

They spoke not a word during the short ride to the school. Runt sat facing forward, Winnie and Ma Cherie trying to look humble and scared, though not needing to try so hard in looking scared.

"Wait here. I won't be long. Then you can take me to the train station," Runt told the cabby, as they got out of the carriage.

Approaching the front gate, the two guards came to attention. They immediately recognized Runt.

"Mr. Runt, it's good to see you, again, sir," they said.

"I have a delivery for Madame," Runt said, gesturing to Winnie and Ma Cherie.

"What's with this one?" asked one of the guards, pointing at Ma Cherie, suggesting Ma Cherie wasn't of the normal Fancy Girl variety.

"She's the new cook," Runt proclaimed. "Man does not live by lust alone," he concluded, laughing at his witticism, the other two men saw no humor in it.

Once through the gate, one of the guards began ushering them to the house.

"That's all right, no need, I know the way," Runt pointed out.

The guard shrugged his shoulders. Thinking this one less task to do, he turned and walked back to the front gate with the other guard.

They entered the house, standing in the empty hallway.

Runt moved toward them, whispering, "Well, I've got you in. It's up to you two, now. I only ask that whatever it is you plan to do that you don't do it till I'm on my way. Give me a minute or two."

Winnie nodded that they would.

Runt turned, walking out of the building to the front gate.

"That was quick," said one of the guards.

"It was just a delivery."

They opened the gate.

"Have a good day, sir," they said as they locked the gate once more.

"See you boys again real soon," Runt called out over his shoulder.

The cabby jumped down to help Runt back into the carriage.

"To the train station, cabby, as quickly as possible..."

They rode off swiftly and just in time, for all hell was about to break loose.

Thirty-Five

Winnie's Escapade

They stood silently in the empty hallway. Suddenly, a child's cry echoed throughout the house. It was coming from the floor above them.

"That's Madame's office," Winnie whispered, pointing to a door halfway down the hall. "I'll go get William."

With that they both reached into their aprons, taking their guns in hand. They started up the hallway. When they got to the office door, Ma Cherie quickly entered, slamming the door behind her.

Winnie continued down the hallway, slowly and cautiously, pointing her pistol in front of her, holding it in her two shaking hands.

She could find no one around. When she got to the parlor, it was empty. Surely, they were upstairs, as was William.

Standing at the foot of the staircase, she looked up to see no one. She secured her gun in one hand, freeing the other to hold onto the banister. Trying her best not to make a sound, she moved her way up the stairs.

At the next landing, she found no one. Her mind flooded with memories, remembering the months she lived and studied at the school to be a Fancy. Two doors from the top of the landing was the door to the bedroom that she and Jolene shared so long ago. Like steel to a magnet, she was drawn to it.

She opened the door slowly in hopes there would be no trouble. To her surprise, there was William, alone.

The child sat on a large quilt spread out on the floor. There were articles around him to keep him amused. Winnie's first emotion was of anger that they would leave the child alone in a room, how unsafe, how careless. Then the feeling went away as Winnie watched her son, slowly, clumsily, working his way to his feet. He smiled at her, clearly in recognition.

She dashed across the room to him. Bending low, she scooped him up in one arm, the other still holding the pistol. Turning, she started for the door, only it was too late.

Cora stood in the doorway, pointing a pistol at Winnie, behind her stood a small group of soon-to-be Fancy Girls.

"Step aside, Cora. I swear I'll kill you," Winnie spat out her words.

On hearing this, the young girls moved out of her aim, running down the hall to other rooms, locking their doors behind them. Cora stood her ground.

"I could say the same to you," Cora laughed. "Only, do you want to take that chance, holding your baby? I'm not like Madame. I don't have a dog in this fight. I couldn't care less if I blow a hole in you or your brat. Toss the gun down, Winnie; place the boy back onto the quilt."

Winnie's mind flooded with thoughts of different scenarios, each racing through her mind. She followed them from beginning to end; each time it ended badly.

She dropped the gun to the floor, raising her hand.

"Kick it across the floor to me," Cora ordered.

Winnie did just that.

"Now, put the baby down."

Again, Winnie did as she was told.

"Keep your hands up; start walking toward me."

When Winnie got to the doorway, Cora backed off, letting her go before her, never taking her aim off Winnie.

"Keep moving slowly," Cora warned. "Now, go downstairs. Just remember, I've got my gun on you, and I'd shot you as soon as spit."

Keeping her hands high, Winnie started slowly down the stairs. For a second time, Winnie's mind swam with scenarios that only led to death. Could she move fast enough, spin around, knocking the gun from Cora's hand? Of course, she couldn't. She could feel the muzzle of the gun pressing hard and sharp at the center of her back.

It was then fate stepped in.

Halfway down the stairs, gunshots rang out, coming from down the hall. They could only assume it was the guards shooting at someone. Then it became a hail of bullets. Not being able to see Cora's gun pressed into Winnie's back, for some reason they were shooting at her and Cora. Some of the bullets hit the steps just below Winnie. Shards of wood flew high and far in every direction.

The explosions took them both by surprise. It was then Winnie felt the muzzle of Cora's gun move from the center of her back. If she had the slightest chance of getting away, now was the time.

Winnie whirled around, taking hold of Cora's hand that held the gun, pointing it upwards, the gun fired, the bullet lodging into the ceiling, sending plaster down on them. Winnie then pulled Cora's arm downward, causing her to fall forward and then down the stairs. Tumbling, Cora hit her head several times, knocking her unconscious.

Looking down on the motionless Cora, Winnie's first thoughts were to reach down, take the gun, rush back upstairs, collect William, and then try to blast her way out. Only, on second thought, as more bullets whizzed about, she knew it was pointless and dangerous for both her and William. Gunshots were tearing into the stair steps above and upper landing. Running upstairs would be futile.

She leaped over Cora, taking a quick right, getting out of the way of gunfire. In the dining room, that's when she remembered how years earlier Jolene tried to scale the outer wall by hopping on one of the dining room chairs pressed against the garden wall. As hard as Jolene tried she was unable to make it over the wall. That's when Jolene asked for her help. With a boost from Winnie, Jolene made it over the wall. It was a long shot, still she had to try.

Winnie took one of the dining room chairs outside, putting it against the outer wall. Like Jolene, she was unable to scale the wall.

In a last-ditch attempt, Winnie went back to the house, turning, began running across the lawn, when she got to the chair, she raised her leg up onto it, vaulting upwards. She grabbed hold of the wall's ledge, using all her strength she made it to the top of the wall and over to the other side.

Realizing there was nothing she could do at the moment, she knew she had to get away, saying a prayer for Ma Cherie, and vowing to return for William.

It confused Winnie. Something wasn't right. As she ran away, she could still hear gunfire. None of the shots taken at her; it was from inside the house. Who was shooting and at whom was a mystery. A block away, she could still hear the gunshots.

She worried for Ma Cherie. Winnie could only hope that she escaped as she did.

Blocks away, she became aware of the people on the streets staring at her. Then she realized why. Of course, they were staring. She was running, huffing and puffing in a cold sweat. She needed to slow down to a normal walk, if she was to be inconspicuous.

She felt lost. She had no idea where she was or what direction she was going. It would be a foolish move to go home, even if she knew how to get there. Then she remembered her promise to Ma Cherie. No matter the outcome, they would rendezvous at the cottage. Only, how would she get to the cottage. It was too far to travel by foot.

Walking on she passed a stable with doors opened wide. She took her time moving passed it, looking inside, there was no one watching over it. There were saddles, bridles, carriages, bags of feed, and of course, horses, except no workers. Perhaps, they abandoned their post to have supper?

"Is there anybody here?" Winnie called out. There was no answer, only the neighing of horses.

She had to act fast. In the back was an older, smaller and calmer looking horse than the others that were clearly younger. It was a gray mare with a white star on its forehead. Taking the horse from its stall, she patted it gently on the neck, trying to make some kind of a connection, trying to keep it composed.

There was a wooden box off to the side. She moved it next to the horse. Placing her right foot on the box, her hand the horse's mane, with one swift push, she was atop of the mare. Perhaps, because she wasn't a heavy person, or the horse's tranquil temperament, or both, the mare gave little to no resistance. With a few gentle kicks in the side, they were out of the stable, racing down the street.

Again, she was drawing attention. People stared at her as she galloped by. Some even pointed at her. After all, here was a young, poorly dressed woman, racing down the street on an old mare, riding bareback, not a sidesaddle, and wearing a full skirt.

A few blocks later, she got her bearings. She was going east; she needed to go north, to the cottage.

****

Celene was up and about, feeling better with each passing day. She planed to return to her apartment at the end of the week.

Philip came to have lunch with them. Once Jolene placed the servings on the table, she joined them. They were just about to say grace when they heard it. They stopped cold, sitting up straight, listening.

Philip was the first to recognize the sound.

"Someone on horseback, riding like the blazes," he said, leaving the table and stepping outside the cottage, followed closely by Jolene and Celene.

They stood in front of the cottage, looking out on the horizon. At first, it was just a dark rider off in the distance. As it grew closer, they could see it was a woman on horseback. Coming closer, Jolene knew who it was.

"My God, it's Winnie. What could be the matter?" Jolene said, stepping forward.

Finally, Winnie came galloping up to them, stopping abruptly. The horse stood panting and lathered in sweat; Winnie was not much worse for wear. She tumbled off the mare, hitting the ground with a thud.

Philip ran out, taking her up in his arms, bringing her into the cottage, placing her on the sofa. He backed away, giving Jolene room to sit next to her. Celene handed a cup of water for Winnie.

Jolene lifted Winnie's head. "Here, take a sip."

She struggled, chocking on the swallow of water.

"Oh, Jolene, all is lost," Winnie said in tears.

"What are you saying? What's happened?"

"I've lost my son; I've lost William. I'm sure to lose Jonathan when he finds out what I've done. I'm sure to be a wanted criminal. I've ruined everything, forever."

"You don't know that," Jolene tried to encourage her.

"No," she insisted. "I've let everyone down. I've ruined everyone's life."

"Not mine," Jolene declared. "My life is better for knowing you."

Philip tapped Jolene on the shoulder, gesturing for her to move, allowing him to take over, and speak.

"Winnie, listen to me." He spoke softly. "Where there is breath, there is still hope. God the Father wants the best for you. Pray to him; he will never let you down."

"He hates me," Winnie replied. "I've let him down."

"No, he could never hate you. It is you who have let you down."

Thirty-Six

Ma Cherie's Escapade

Ma Cherie rushed into the office, slamming the door behind her, leaning her back against it, holding her pistol aimed at Madame Charbonneau.

To Ma Cherie's surprise, Madame Charbonneau smiled, hardly blinking an eye.

"I know you," Madame declared. "You're Mrs. Gibbs' woman."

"Where's the child?" Ma Cherie insisted.

Madame laughed at her. "You think you can just come in here waving a gun around? My men will kill you before you can blink."

"You think that frightens me?" Ma Cherie snarled.

Madame looked deep into her eyes. "No, I don't believe you're frightened. Then again, I don't particularly fear you, either. So, what do you propose we do about this stand off?"

Madame began laughing into Ma Cherie's face; the sound of it was demon-like, sending terror up and down her spine, like the flow of hot lava.

Something was wrong. Things weren't going as planned. Even with a gun in her hand, Ma Cherie did not feel like the one in charge, she had no control over the matter, Madame did.

Mixed with panic, strange thoughts flew through her mind, evil thoughts. How could someone go from being a God-fearing woman, reading the Bible, praying day and night, following the Golden Rule, become a murderer?

Well, not quite a murderer, yet. All that she need do was to pull the trigger, which she was certain she was going to do. That's what scared her. She knew without a doubt she was going to pull the trigger. She delighted in the idea. She found pleasure in it.

At least, there was no begging for mercy from Madame. That would make things harder, yet not impossible. In fact, Madame's defiant attitude was making it easier for Ma Cherie.

"Do you want to pray before I kill you?"

"You still believe in that mumbo jumbo?" she laughed

"You should try to get right with the Lord, before I send you to him. You've done much evil in your life."

"True, but I've never killed anyone, not directly, that is." Again, Madame laughed.

Those words cut the deepest.

"Go on, I'm waiting. Go ahead, pull the trigger!" Madame sneered.

A long silent moment took hold of them, constricting the breath from their bodies.

"You're not going to kill me," Madame announced, sounding amused.

"Why won't I?"

"Because I know your type and I know you. I remember when first seeing you. I said, 'There's another sad-eyed country girl'. Just look at you, I'd say you haven't changed much since your early days as a young girl on the plantation. I know your type. You're one of those holier-than-thou sorts. Butter wouldn't melt in your mouth. Looking down your nose at all of us sinners, only, now you see you're no different from the rest of us. You're capable of murder, as much as the next person. Except, in your mind you don't realize it, you're still on a spiritual quest. So, you won't kill me. You think you're a saint, well, saints don't kill people!"

Her argument seemingly fell on deaf ears.

"You know, if you kill me, they'll hang you!"

"I've cheated death many times, and you know what happened, then? I've been living on borrowed time, since. I'm prepared to die."

She pulled back on the gun hammer till it clicked into place.

"Now, wait a minute," Madame's voice quivered, "can't we talk this over?"

"There's nothing to talk over. Unless you can perform miracles, there's nothing you can do to make it right."

"Now, wait one damn minute!"

Ma Cherie closed her eyes, pulling the trigger. The gunshot sounded through the house like a cannon blast, echoing from room to room and ricocheting back. She'd never fired a gun in her life. The explosion surprised and shocked her. The recoil sent her arm behind her.

The body hit the floor with a loud thud. It lay lifeless behind the desk. Blood collected around the head, slowly forming a large pool around the body. The crimson splatter was across one wall, masking the titles of the books on the shelf of another wall, and a red spray across a painting of the same woman she just shot, only when she was young.

The guards were sure to have heard. They would come soon. If she was going to do anything, she needed to do it without hesitation.

Then she thought of her options. There were only three. She could make a run for it. Her chances of escaping were slim to none, and she knew it. Even if it were possible, she'd have to move immediately. Or she could give herself up, which would surely lead to her arrest, jailing, trial, and eventually hanging, if they didn't just shoot her at that moment. She also had the notion she might try to fight her way out. She still had five bullets. Except, they outnumbered her, eclipsed by men who knew how to use a gun far better than she, the best she could hope for was taking one or two of them with her. This she felt was a worthless gesture.

She heard their heavy feet trampling through the house like cattle; the pounding on the wood floor was all around. Then shots rang out. She feared they had gotten Winnie.

Then as if a bolt of lightning hit her, she thought of one more unexpected alternative. She placed the gun to the side of her head.

Her gun hand shook. She was just about to pull the trigger when the office door swung open. To her surprise, it wasn't the guards. It was Jonathan, gun in one hand, William on his hip, held in his other arm.

"Ma Cherie, we need to go, now!" he shouted.

It was as if the words floated slowly across the room, poured into her ears where they lodged, never making it to her brain. She stood still, as if in shock, her eyes wide, the muzzle of her gun pressed against the side of her head.

Jonathan leaped across the room. With his gun hand, he slapped the gun from her hand, just as the gun fired, sending the bullet into the wall.

It was then they heard a moan coming from the floor. It came from Madame. With closer inspection, it was clear she wasn't dead. Ma Cherie's shaky hand only caused a deep bloody gash in the side of Madame's head.

"She's not dead! Thank God," Ma Cherie claimed aloud, feeling relieved.

"Here, take William," Jonathan said, handing William to her. The poor child looked around in confusion, too afraid to cry.

Jonathan made sure he had Ma Cherie's attention. "Stay close, and stay behind me at all times," he ordered as he picked up her pistol from the floor.

Ma Cherie nodded, following him across the room and out of the office. In the hallway, bullets flew. The guards were at one end of the hallway, near the front door. Jonathan fired back, both guns blazing, working his way back down the hall, Ma Cherie and William behind him.

When they got to the parlor, they turned rushing into the dining room, out the French doors to the backyard.

Jonathan remembered all too well the stories Winnie told him about helping Jolene over the garden wall using a chair. If it were possible, it didn't matter at this moment, not with an old woman and a baby.

There was no alternative other than to go to the front of the house, where the guards waited, and try to shoot their way out.

"Stay close behind me," Jonathan once more cautioned Ma Cherie.

They moved warily along the side of the house till they came to the front lawn. There were three guards in the doorway of the front door, two stood shooting wildly down the hallway, and the third lay on the ground, presumably dead.

Holding William tightly, Ma Cherie rushed to the front gate, which they left unguarded. Jonathan moved in the same direction, only backwards and slowly, keeping both guns aimed at the guards. Thankfully, their constant gunfire drowned out any noise Ma Cherie and Jonathan made.

However, the gun blasts were too freighting for a small child. William began crying. His wailing was not louder than the gunfire, however significantly different. Noticing something unusual in the air, one of the guards looked behind, he tapped the other guard on the shoulder. They both spun around and started firing.

"Run!" Jonathan shouted.

Ma Cherie was only a few feet from the open gate. She held her breath, racing off the property and down the road.

Jonathan was only halfway to the gate. Walking backwards, firing both his guns in succession. He was able to hit both guards, one in the arm, causing him to drop his gun, the other square in the chest. When the shooting stopped, he ran through the gate, running down the road. In little time, he caught up with Ma Cherie. Poor frightened William was still crying.

"Are you all right?" Jonathan asked.

"I'm fine, so is the baby," Ma Cherie replied. "We need to get to Winnie. She's at a cottage just outside town."

"Yes, I know it," Jonathan said to Ma Cherie's surprise. "We could never get there on horseback, especially with William."

Again, Ma Cherie sounded stunned. "You know about William?"

"I've known for some time now," he responded

"Winnie loves you," Ma Cherie added, feeling it needed saying.

"I know that," he said.

"Then why...?" Ma Cherie asked in confusion.

"Because, I love her," he countered, and then reaching out to William placing his hand on his cheek. "William, my son," he whispered, gently. William stopped crying.

Ma Cherie took a moment to look at Jonathan walking at her side.

"My God, Jonathan, you've been hit!"

Thirty-Seven

Rendezvous at the Cottage

"How is she?" Jolene asked Celene sitting next to Winnie, cooling her brow with a damp towel.

"Much better, she's asleep."

"The poor dear, so much sorrow has come to her," Jolene whispered.

"Most of it brought on by her own hand," Celene added.

Jolene didn't say anything, knowing the truth of the statement.

"Let her rest. Sleep is a fragrant rose that hides away the sadness of life's misfortunes, even though it's only for a night, it's still welcomed," Celene said, rising from her chair to bring the towel to the kitchen.

The three of them stayed far from the sofa, not to disturb Winnie.

"I keep rattling my brain about what we can do to help," Jolene said, "but all I can think of is prayer."

"There's nothing wrong with or stronger than prayer, my love," Philip said, reaching for his wife's hand.

"I know, God forgive me, I feel like I need to do something."

This time it was Celene who heard the distant sound.

"Someone's coming. Do you hear it? It sounds like a wagon," Celene said, walking to the front door, followed by Jolene and Philip.

Opening the door, they stood in the entrance, looking out beyond the fields. A dust cloud whirled low in the sky, indicating it was either a group of horsemen, or as Celene thought – a wagon.

As it approached, it was clear it was an open carriage. Coming closer, they could see the driver riding on top and someone sitting in the carriage.

When it was less than a quarter mile away, they were in for a shock. The driver was none other than Ma Cherie and the passenger was Jonathan.

"Oh, my God, it's Ma Cherie and Jonathan!" Jolene exclaimed, perhaps louder than she should have.

Those words drifted into the cottage, hovered over Winnie for an átomos of a second, then soared into land of her subconscious. There they echoed in her mind loud enough to wake her.

Leaping from the sofa, she rushed to the front door, pushing the others aside, stepping outside into the slowly dimming light of a brilliant sunset.

Ma Cherie pulled back on the reins, slowing the carriage down. Her facial features became more distinct, as they approached. There was no elation seen in her eyes, stern lines dug deep into her features, an expression of forlorn and hopelessness. This was not going to be a joyous occasion. This was without a doubt a tragedy in the making.

When they were only a few feet away, Winnie could see Jonathan sitting in the back of the carriage. His expression was no different from that of Ma Cherie, if not more somber. A dark cloud of gloom hung over the carriage.

It was then Winnie could see that Jonathan was holding something in front of him, against his chest. When Winnie realized it was William he was holding, she took off running to the carriage. Ma Cherie halted the carriage no more than twenty feet from the cottage. The others followed close behind Winnie.

In the short moment, the run from cottage to carriage, a hundred thoughts swam through her mind. It was obvious Jonathan knew about his son, which meant he also knew about her lies. Would he accept William? Knowing Jonathan the way she did, she assumed he would. Still, it would mean a great sacrifice he'd have to make, would he?

Worst of all, would he still love her, after all the dishonesty? Would he turn his back on her? She couldn't blame him if he did.

Finally, when she was standing next to the carriage, next to Jonathan, she reached out to them.

"William!" she cried, placing her hand on the child, grabbing him from the waist.

"No...Don't...Not yet," Jonathan said in a low moan. "Let me hold him for a little longer."

This took Winnie aback. She looked up at Ma Cherie. There were tears streaming from her eyes down her checks.

She looked again at William. Was the child asleep? For a moment, Winnie feared the worst till William moved about in his father's arms, letting out a long sigh. The sight of his tiny back rising and falling with breath comforted her.

The others remained only an earshot behind Winnie, wanting to give them all the time and space they needed.

With tear soaked eyes, Winnie looked to Jonathan.

Jonathan's hands held William tightly and close, gently caressing the boy. He looked at her, his eyes clearly red from crying.

"Why?" he asked softly.

The word plunged deep into Winnie's heart like a dagger. She stood there lost for words.

"Do you not know how much I love you? Do you not know how I love what comes from our love? This is my son, he's beautiful. Why would you think I wouldn't love him?"

"I was afraid for your career," she answered softly and shamefully.

"Winnie, I would give my life for my family. Losing my life couldn't compared to losing you and this sweet child."

"Can you ever forgive me," she asked.

"Of course, I forgive you." he said tenderly.

Just then, William began to wake, stirring in his father's arms.

"Here, you best take him, now," Jonathan said, releasing his hold of William, kissing his son one last time.

Winnie reached out, taking William.

"Oh, my God, Jonathan, you're hurt!" she screamed in terror.

It was true; his front was covered in blood, his shirt crimson, as was the front of William's clothing.

"Take my breath away with one last kiss," he whispered.

Winnie was shaking and crying. She turned handing William to Jolene. Slowly, she crept up the side of the carriage. Reaching out, she took hold of Jonathan's arms. Too weak to move on his own, she placed his arms about her shoulders. Leaning forward, she placed her lips to his. For a moment, she felt his lips pressing against hers, his breath warm on her upper lip. Then the breath became a sigh, long and slow till it was gone. With that, his lips went limp as did his arms.

Winnie fell on top of him, crying frantically. Behind her, she heard William begin crying, also. She turned, reaching out for him. Jolene gently gave William to her.

"He's gone, Jolene! Jonathan is gone!"

Thirty-Eight

Epilogue

Gossip is like an ocean wave. It crashes to the shoreline with great force; it slowly dissipates, and then is gone forever, never to be seen again.

For weeks, everyone in New Orleans talked about the missing Judge Gibbs and his wife, Winifred. He was the top contender to run for mayor. Now, he was nowhere to be found. Was there foul play? They made an extensive investigation, which turned up nothing.

After a month, no one talked about the Gibbs, and in time, no one cared, that is except Bernard Addison. The man was born with suspicion in his blood, and a six-sense for clues. It didn't take him long to put the pieces together. Yet, once he'd learned the truth, he decided it would do nobody any good to learn it. So, he kept it to himself, swearing to take it to his grave.

As for Madame Charbonneau, she recovered nicely. Though the wound to her skull left a deep scare, her plentiful, long dark hair kept it hidden. Concerning the escapade, she chalked it up as a loss. After replacing a few items, cleaning up the bloodstains, plastering over the bullet holes, and hiring new guards, it was business as usual.

****

It would seem Ma Cherie was not the only one in the Gibbs' household with their ear to the doors, peering through keyholes. After Addison warned him of the goings-on, Jonathan began to probe deeper. Eventually, there wasn't anything about the circumstances he didn't know. Though, he felt tempted on many occasion to confront his wife, he never did, always believing in the love he shared with Winnie, trusting that in time it would all work out.

They buried Jonathan at the foot of the large tree, on the edge of the wood where Philip and Jolene would picnic with William. This way all felt he was a part of the picnics they had later, which included Ma Cherie, Celene, and of course, Winnie.

Winnie never returned to New Orleans, determined to start her life anew, and raise her William as best she could. She declined offers from Jolene and Philip to move into the cottage with them. She found residence in a small abandoned cabin not far away. It was in ruins when she moved in, however with the help of the others it was a cozy, warm home for her and William.

Though Winnie swore she could never love another man as she did Jonathan, seven years later she began courting one of the single men at church. Stanley R. Smith was a good kindly man. And although Winnie told him she would never love a man as much as her first marriage, believing some love is better than none, the two wed. He was an excellent husband to Winnie and a father to William.

The situation with Ma Cherie was a strange one. For days, she complained she no longer felt she fit anywhere, feeling out of place, out of sorts. Till one day, she got it in her head to leave. They tried to talk her out of it, telling her how much they loved and needed her, yet she would not be swayed. She remained determined to leave. One by one she made her good-byes. There were kisses mixed with tears. With the morning light, she was gone, never to be heard from again.

Celene moved back into her apartment in the back of the church. She kept busy with church work and her new family. A sweet natured woman, pleasant to look upon, she was never short of interested men. Only, for some reason the pieces never quite fit. It looked as if she would spend her life alone. However, that was not to be, as we will soon see.

Jolene and Philip remained at the cottage. Their love for each other became legendary throughout the county. Their love at the time of their wedding, as beautiful as it was, could only be described as a flower bud. In years, it blossomed to a beauty admired and envied by all who met them.

They worked hard for the church, taking little time for them; however that was the way they wanted it. Like Abram and Sarah, it began to seem too late in life for them to have children, however, Jolene was with child. Never was there a happier couple.

He was a June baby, dark like his father. They named him Seth. Jolene spent most of her day with the child, loving on him and teaching him. Seth grew fast from the country air, inheriting a gentle and sweet manner from his mother, and to be brave, wise, and reverent like his dad.

Seth was three years younger than William, looking up to him as an older brother. When they were in their teens the two boys were close, both handsome, looking very much alike, they called each other cousin. Even then, Seth played the younger brother, following William around like a lost puppy.

Stanley R. Smith, gladly or sadly, depending on your point of view, received an offer for a good job in another state. Plans were made, promises sworn, nevertheless in time they lost all contact. Jolene and Winnie were never to see each other again.

They said it was the coldest winter on record. It seemed like it would never stop snowing. Everything was covered in white for months. Many people fell sick. It was Reverend Philip's duty to visit the sick and bury the dead. For months, he went about the county visiting the ailing, it was mostly the older ones who suffered the most and died. After months, of tramping through the snow, going to visit the sick and the dying, it all finally caught up with Philip. He was bedridden with pneumonia.

When his lungs filled up with fluid, there was nothing they could do other than make him comfortable. Three days later he died in Jolene's arms. Seth, now a young man, dealt with his sorrow by walking the mountain trails, keeping to himself. They buried Philip under the picnic tree, where they buried Jonathan.

Some say to die of a broken heart is the saddest death of all. Philip's death destroyed Jolene from the inside out. She knew better. She knew she still had a son to raise and love. Yet, to go on was impossible. It would be like asking her to pull the arrow out of her heart and carry on. It would only make matters worse.

In the spring, with her loved ones, Seth and Celene, at her bedside, Jolene breathed her last. Before doing so, she made Celene vow she would finish raising Seth till he became a man. Celene gladly swore she would.

Holding Seth's hand on one side and Celene's hand on the other, she spoke her last word, 'Philip'.

They buried her next to her beloved Philip under the picnic tree. From then on, they seldom went to the picnic spot, since now, all those considered family were gone, either to places unknown or to the grave. Still, Celene and Seth would picnic once a year under the tree in the springtime, on the anniversary of Jolene's passing.

****

As for the young men, William and Seth, they grew to full manhood, and to follow different paths.

William's life was a sad one. No matter how much love his mother, Winnie, showered him with or how well his stepfather treated him, the weight of the past was always too much to bear. Never knowing much about his true father frustrated him. The rejection he felt, possibly as far back as in his mother's womb caused a bend in him leading him down the path of anger and rebellion. As an adult, he always picked the wrong friends and the wrong course. Always he lived on the wrong side of the law, on the road to perdition.

Now, Seth was different, his parents with the help of his Aunt Celene raised him well. He was a man everyone respected and loved. Born with an inquisitive mind, he read every book he could get his hands on, feeding his soul and his heart.

Finally, the day came, as it does for all young men, Seth set out to make his mark on the world. He swore that when he made good, he would send for his Auntie Celene. Then he could take care of her.

True to his word, a time came when he did well, respected and wealthy, making that deep mark on the world as he intended. However, that is a story for another day.

THE END

Michael Edwin Q. is available for book interviews and personal appearances. For more information contact:

Michael Edwin Q.
michaeledwinq.com

Other Titles in this series by Michael Edwin Q:

Born A Colored Girl: 978-1-59755-478-4
Pappy Moses' Peanut Plantation: 978-1-59755-482-8
But Have Not Love: 978-1-59755-494-7
Tame the Savage Heart: 978-1-59755-5098
A Slaves Song: 978-1-59755-527-5
Fancy: 978-1-59755-540-1
Wistful:978-1-59755-563-0
Winnie:978-1-59755-6002

To purchase additional copies of these books visit our bookstore website at:
www.advbookstore.com

Longwood, Florida, USA
"we bring dreams to life"™
www.advbookstore.com

Made in the USA
Las Vegas, NV
04 February 2023

66914229R00095